The Puppet Hunter

First paperback edition May 2025

Book cover design by Nihkri@fiverr

ISBN 978-1-7367559-6-9 (paperback)
ISBN 978-1-7367559-7-6 (ebook)

www.trisharrowsmithauthor.com

Character List

Carlson
Walt- Post Master
Sally- Bakery Owner
Roy (17)

Chambers
Randy- Bank Manager
June- Diner Owner
Bobby (17)
Sarah (15)

Peters
Colton- Hardware
Store Co-owner
Kimberley- SaHM
Oscar (15)
Josh (18)
Beth-Ann (17)

Sheridan
Jim- Farmer
Suzanne- Farmer
Clint (18)
Kelsey (17)
Jimmy (15)

Sutton
Ely- Bar Owner
Emily- Bar Owner
Mary-Jane (17)
Sue-Ellen (15)

Walker
Rex- Sheriff
Marilyn- SaHM
Lizbeth (17)

Bill Allen- Grocery Store Owner
Frank Anderson- Fireman
Maris Brown- Retired
Cyrus Harper- Hardware Store Co-owner
Jake Grant- Pharmacist
Ruth Richards- Hotel Owner
Tim Williams- Reverend

Chapter I

My masterpiece is complete and what a beautiful sight it has become.

CURRENT DAY

Flames licked the side of the cabinet, grasping for the corner of the kitchen curtains. Bobby lifted the metal trash can with gloved hands, enough to encourage the flames to go higher. He let it slip from his grasp, scattering the remaining contents across the floor, and grabbed a hand towel from the counter. He took a deep breath, regretting it as smoke filled his lungs. Leaning forward, he dipped the edge of the towel into the expanding fire and threw it towards the nearest corner before walking out the door.

Dry leaves crunched under his feet, the crisp, autumn breeze bit at his skin through his sweatshirt and jeans. He longed, for a moment, to be nearer to the flames again. Shivering, he remembered how warm the evenings had been mere weeks before. Fall moved in quickly this year, the cooler weather adding a hazy veil to the already desolate feeling within the community.

Bobby stood outside the window, watching the intimate dance between the smoke and flames, awed by how beautiful it would be if it weren't so destructive. He pulled his phone from his pocket and dialed the emergency number to report the fire. He wasn't an arsonist, but this was the only way he could get the sheriff to listen. He knew the girls were in this house and he was willing to do whatever it took to save them, even if it meant giving up his own freedom.

TEN HOURS EARLIER

Every morning started the same as today. He entered the room singing about walking on sunshine in a dull monotone. His presence made me want to hide, cower in a corner until he moved on, but I couldn't move. Suspended in the air, the ropes around my arms and legs held me in the same position for hours. I squinted hard against the sudden onslaught of track lighting while he pulled the curtains to the side to reveal a crudely drawn sun. Shaded in yellow and orange crayon, scotch tape held the paper to the brick wall in the makeshift window. He'd attached rough cut pieces of cardboard to the brick to create the illusion of a window frame and sill. Laughable, if not for the situation.

"Mother always told me to start each day by welcoming the sun but you, my dear puppet, bring me more warmth and light than the sun ever has."

My skin prickled as he drew his finger down the side of my face and over my lips. A slow moan rose from his throat. His tongue slid across his own lips, leaving them glistening with saliva. Dangling at the perfect height for him, he grasped my sides and pulled my body against his, slowly pressing his hips into mine. Feeling his arousal, I closed my eyes and tried to pretend I was anywhere else. His grip loosened and I swung backward, the ropes tearing into the skin on my wrists.

One by one, he turned the four wooden cranks on the wall which lowered me to the floor. The process was the same each day. I knew he would change my dress and I secretly hoped the one he chose would have a zippered back. I could always feel the caress of both hands as the zipper went up or down, but it was better than the alternative of the corset style where his hands lingered too long while he laced up the front and tightened the strings. During every dress change, he found an excuse, something to adjust, that allowed him to touch every part of exposed flesh. The smile on his face and the look in his eyes told me he enjoyed every moment.

Bobby stormed into the Sheriff's office, sweating and out of breath. Half his flannel shirt had come untucked and chestnut hair stuck out in clumps, making it look like he had just woken up. He doubled over and rested his palms on his knees.

Rex stared at him, not happy about his sudden appearance. If he wasn't here to turn himself in, there wasn't a reason Rex could think of for his presence. He remained seated and silent, waiting for Bobby to speak.

Through ragged breaths, Bobby blurted out, "I know where the girls are." He seemed convinced of himself, but the sheriff wasn't so sure.

Twice already, Rex had pulled Bobby in for questioning. It made sense that he would try to blame someone else for the girls' disappearances. He thought he might have done the same thing if he were in Bobby's position. But now, at his age and with his background and training, he saw nothing but guilt with the way Bobby was acting. "Bobby, I don't think you should be here. Why don't you go back to school?"

"No. I know where they are. You need to come with me so I can show you." He finally managed to stand up straight after catching his breath.

"Did you see them? How do you know for sure where they are?" Rex still hadn't moved from his spot behind his desk. He was busy preparing an excuse for whatever Bobby came up with for a response.

"Well, no. I didn't actually see them, but I didn't have to. I can lead you straight to them."

The sheriff finally stood. He walked over to Bobby and rested his hand on his shoulder. "Unless they are on your property and you're giving me permission to search it, I'm going to need you to go back to school. Now."

"Of course they're not on my property. I told you I didn't take them. Do you think I'm stupid?" He stared at Rex with a look of defiance on his face. He was young, but he wasn't dumb.

"No, Bobby. I don't think you're stupid at all. But you are still a suspect. You need to keep your nose out of other people's business and leave the police work to me." He opened the door and gave Bobby a gentle, guided push through the opening. "Go to school and stay out of trouble."

As the door closed behind him, Bobby turned and shouted. "Leave the police work to you? I know where the girls are. I'm a better detective than you are."

Rex took a deep breath and let it out slowly, trying to rid himself of the desire to open the door and yell back. Instead, he made his way back to his desk and sank into his chair.

Martin, the head detective from the next city over, leaned against the door frame of the interrogation room, chewing on a toothpick. "You're not going to follow him?"

Rex squinted and his top lip curled. "No, I'm not going to follow him. There's a ninety-nine percent chance he's going straight to school, one percent he'll go home."

The detective shifted the toothpick from one side of his mouth to the other with his tongue. "What makes you so sure about that?"

Still annoyed that he had to ask for outside help, Rex was hesitant to entertain any of Martin's questions. From the moment they walked through the door, Martin and Parker treated Rex like he was incompetent. The truth was simply that the case was more involved than Rex and his one deputy were able to handle on their own. It didn't mean he was incapable of doing his job. "Listen, Bobby's a good kid. He causes trouble every now and again, but he's a teenager. That's what they're supposed to do."

"So, you think because he's a teenager, all the evidence you have against him is null and void?"

"I think anything I try to pin on him would be considered circumstantial, at best." He picked up a pen and started tapping it anxiously on his desk. His foot followed the same rhythm. "We've brought him in twice. We questioned him together twice. We let him go twice. Why are you so convinced that it's him?"

"Because it's him."

Rex sighed and rolled his eyes, his pen keeping a steady beat on the desk. "And yet, you haven't arrested him yet."

Martin sighed. "You can do what you want, this is your town. But you're going to be sorry when we catch him. And we will catch him. You only think people don't like you know, wait until they find out the truth and realize you did nothing to stop it." He spit the toothpick into the nearest trash can and retreated to the interrogation room that had become their makeshift office.

Being such a small town, the police station didn't need to be large. It contained two holding cells, primarily used as drunk tanks for out-of-town visitors who had nothing better to do than cause trouble. The interrogation room was useless most days and had become more of a storage area than anything else. Rex didn't have his own office. His desk sat off to the side of the main room, opposite his secretary. The only other desk took up the middle, facing the front door. Rex always thought that should be the desk his secretary used but she wouldn't have it. She argued about having the wall space to hang her calendar and bulletin board. The walls were a muddy white and the paint started chipping near the ceiling years ago. Until six months ago, they had plenty of spare time to repaint the building both inside and out but there didn't seem to be any point. Only three people ever saw it long enough to pay attention and none of them cared about the flaws.

Rex stood and walked over to the interrogation room. He poked his head through the open doorway and tapped on the glass to get the team's attention. "I'm going out for a bit. I have my cell." He heard one of the detectives call out behind him.

"Good to know, but you won't need it."

He shook his head at the sound of snickering behind him as he slammed the door shut. He felt like he was working with a bunch of children; playground bullies who were trying to exert their power over the weaker of the species. He wasn't comfortable from the beginning, admitting he needed help, but he didn't believe he would regret his decision so deeply. He had lost control of his station and for a while, it was fine. Now that his own daughter was involved, he would appreciate a little sympathy and understanding. For the first time in twenty years, he could honestly say he hated his job.

He didn't have a plan when he left, he just needed to move, to see something different than the four walls that were beginning to suffocate him. Rex didn't have any more leads, the rest of his team wouldn't talk to him unless it was absolutely necessary, and half the town hated him. He was at a loss. He felt so helpless and for the first time ever, he felt useless in his own town. Dunmeyer didn't have a high crime rate, but he was always confident in his abilities to handle whatever may come his way.

He drove aimlessly around town for three hours hoping to find someone he could stop and chat with. No one was out milling about and since the kids were back in school, the streets were quiet. The town always died down when school was in session. Now, with all the girls missing, even the parents with young children were keeping them locked up tight in the safety of their homes. Toward the end of summer, the teenagers stopped having parties, they weren't causing any trouble or partaking in their usual shenanigans. Part was due to their parents having stricter rules, the other because the children themselves were afraid. Those old enough to understand were scared, both males and females alike. They heard news reports all the time of children going missing, but to have it happen in their own town had everyone on edge.

Rex pulled off to the side of the road in front of the diner. He was tired of driving around, looking for anything that caught his eye, and he needed a fresh cup of coffee. He sat in his truck for nearly ten minutes before turning off the engine and hyping himself up to have the courage to walk in. It was all for naught as the diner had only two patrons plus the owner.

"Hey, sheriff. Time for a coffee break?" June smiled at him as politely as she always does.

Thankfully, she was one of the few who hadn't turned on him yet. He walked to the counter and sat on one of the old, wooden stools. "It sure is. I feel like it's been one long, continuous day for months now."

June nodded in agreement and slid a steaming mug of coffee across the counter followed by a plate of lemon meringue pie. "I know it's your favorite. It's on me today."

Rex wrapped both his hands around his coffee mug and his eyes slowly scanned the diner. There was music playing on the overhead speakers but was barely audible even in the absence of other diners and lack of conversation. Like his own station, the diner was in desperate need of repair, or possibly a little updating. The windows had a permanent layer of grunge along the edges and the bottom pane of one of the doors had a crack that had been there as long as he could remember. The tops of most of the stools had splintered and would catch your clothes or your skin if you weren't careful. The lightly padded benches of the booths were a typical, nauseating green vinyl that had worn thin and ripped open throughout the years. The counter's edge had gouges taken out and there was a constant draft in the air with no telltale source of the disturbance.

June didn't say anything, but Rex could see by the look on her face that she was worried about him. He knew he looked terrible. He hadn't slept, he'd been stressed and worried. After months of feeling like he was getting nowhere, it was beginning to take its toll. "It's okay, June. I know how bad I look." He attempted to smile but was aware it was lacking any genuine quality.

She walked around the counter and sat on a stool next to him. She rested her hand on his knee. "Rex, listen. Not citizen to sheriff, but friend to friend, you need to let yourself breathe. I know you're scared. I know you want to do right by everyone, but you should know, better than anyone else in this town, that will never happen. Even those who are seemingly against you know that you're doing everything you can to help those girls. You can't take their anger at face value. They're scared, too. Everyone knows it's not your fault. And now, most of them feel so terrible about the things they said to you, they can't bring themselves to apologize. It may be hard to understand, but if you were in their position, you would probably feel the same way. You're doing a great job and honestly, I don't know how you've managed to keep going this long. I'm proud of you for your determination. I know Marilyn is proud of you, too." She patted his knee before standing up. "Stop beating yourself up over something you can't control. It doesn't help anyone."

She walked back around the counter and busied herself with preparations before the dinner guests arrived. Since the first girl went missing, Ruth had the hotel booked solid every night and the local businesses, including the diner, were booming because of the curious guests. As soon as word got out that a small town girl disappeared, people flocked into town for no reason other than simple curiosity. The days were quiet while the kids were in school but once it turned late afternoon, the town came alive again.

Rex knew she was right. He was both saddened and uplifted by her short speech. He was glad he still had friends left in this town and he hoped people would begin to come around again after he caught the kidnapper. That was how he had to refer to the person taking their children, a kidnapper. He couldn't bring himself to think it was a murderer he was looking for. It was too much for him to bear. He sipped his coffee slowly and took his time trying to savor the meringue. June was right, it was his favorite, but he couldn't enjoy anything knowing that the suspect was still out there. He couldn't find pleasure in anything knowing that teenagers were scared, helpless, and alone. He pushed his half-empty plate away, left a few dollars on the table, enough to cover the coffee and the pie, and walked out without saying a word to anyone.

He stopped at home hoping he would be able to talk to his wife for a few minutes. After all these years just hearing her voice made him feel much better. She always made him feel safe and validated. Marilyn supported him with every decision he made even if it was one she didn't agree with. To him, she was the perfect wife, his best friend, and he couldn't have asked for a better mother for their daughter, Lizbeth.

At the thought of his daughter, his eyes filled with tears. He had let her down in the worst possible way. Even if she were able to find it within herself to forgive him, he would never be able to forgive himself. He pulled into their gravel driveway and was disappointed to see that his wife's car wasn't there. He debated whether to stay for a while or go back to the station. He decided he wasn't quite ready to go back, so he turned off the engine and walked down to empty the mailbox.

His home felt eerily quiet. It was rare that he was there by himself. He dropped the mail on the table, grabbed a can of soda from the refrigerator, and sank into a chair. He rested his forehead in the palm of his hand, closed his eyes, and tried some breathing exercises to calm himself down. It was a practice he found himself doing often over the past few months.

When he felt his muscles ease up a bit, he opened his eyes and noticed what looked like the corner of a postcard sticking out of the pile of mail. He assumed it was junk, but it piqued his curiosity enough for him to pull it out.

He read it twice before slamming his fist on the table. He left his house so fast he didn't even close the door behind him. His tires spit up gravel as he swung his truck around and raced toward the station.

When he arrived, he didn't take the time to turn his truck off. He stomped up to the door, swung it open, and growled into the station. "You all think this is funny?" He slammed the postcard on the desk and waited for one of them to reply. He was breathing heavily from the lack of respect and blatant disregard for his position.

Parker, the small, mousy detective, picked up the card and read it aloud. "Your time is running out." He handed it to Martin and stared at Rex. "First of all, sheriff, none of us did this. Second, where did you get this?"

"From my mailbox. No postmark, so it's obviously someone who knows where I live and it was mixed in so whoever it was put it there within the last two hours."

Martin was busy chewing on a new toothpick and flipping the card back and forth. "Looks like a child wrote this. You don't recognize the writing?"

"Obviously not. I thought it was one of you playing what you thought was a joke." Rex didn't like Martin, but he found Parker insufferable. For being a grown man, he bordered on petite. His ears stuck out at the top and his nose was small and pointed, like a mouse. Rex believed he was mad at the world and tried to use his attitude to make up for what he lacked in stature.

"Like Parker said, it wasn't us. Neither of us left here after you did." He set the card on the desk and spun it around with the tip of his finger. "How many people have access to the hotel comment cards?"

Rex rolled his eyes and dropped onto the chair behind his desk. "Everyone has access to them. We're a small town, remember? I'm pretty sure everyone has written on one at one point or another." He put his elbows on the table and pressed the heels of his hands into his forehead.

Parker began pacing. "Well, that doesn't narrow things down at all. If everyone has access that means it could still be anyone who lives here or any guest that has stayed in the hotel."

Rex slowly lifted his head, his lips curled up in disgust.

Martin cocked his head to the side and was a bit slack-jawed. "Thank you, Captain Obvious, for that little bit of insight. That certainly added a lot to our discussion." He laid his palms flat on the desk. "Well, if it was delivered, as you say, in the last two hours, let's go see who took a break from work during that time frame. We can at least narrow down some residents."

Rex's chair scraped against the floor. "Why don't you guys start next door? I'll go over to the hotel and we can meet in the middle." The other two men muttered in agreement as they all made their way out of the station. "Call me if you find anything out, huh?"

Both men rolled their eyes and Martin replied wile slipping into the driver's seat. "Yes, sheriff. You'll be the first one to know." The annoyance was clear in his voice.

Rex grumbled as he climbed into his truck. Aside from wanting this case solved, he also wanted these men gone. He thought having them here would relieve some of the stress he was feeling, but it made it worse.

He parked his truck in the hotel parking lot and hesitated before getting out. Unlike June, Ruth had made it known that she's not happy with how he has chosen to pursue potential suspects. But he also knows how she is and if he did things the opposite way, she would find fault in that as well.

The bell chimed when he pushed the front door open. Ruth turned around with a smile on her face, ready to greet her guest, until she saw who it was. Her smile immediately fell and she turned her back on him to continue her task.

"Good afternoon, Ruth."

"Sheriff." She had no emotion in her voice and it was clear that she was not planning on entertaining anything he had to say.

Rex audibly sighed. "I just have a few questions and I'll be out of here."

She dropped her arms to her side to dramatize her annoyance and turned her head just enough so he could see the side of her face but said nothing.

He took his spiral notebook and pen out of his shirt pocket and flipped the cover open. "How closely were you watching your guests this afternoon?" Rex watched her body tense up as she turned to face him.

"Sheriff, I'd love to do your job, too, but in case you haven't noticed, I have a hotel to run. I don't have time to babysit my guests."

She had a stern look om her face and Rex couldn't decide whether to be angry or laugh at her attempt to be intimidating. He took two inconspicuous deep breaths before replying. "Ruth. All I need is a straight answer without the sarcastic comments. I already know how you feel, I don't need the attitude. Did you notice any guests leaving the hotel between twelve-thirty and two-thirty today?"

"What time is it now?"

He flipped his wrist up to look at his watch. "It's four twenty-five."

Ruth held one finger up in the air. "Hold on, let me check my sign out sheet..." She rifled through a stack of papers on the top of her desk. "...Oh, that's right. I don't have one. Are we done now?"

"Thank you for your time, Ms. Richards."

He was halfway through the parking lot when his phone rang. "Walker."

"It's Martin. We have a fire."

"Where?" Rex stepped up his speed to a slow run.

"The big house on Maple. The one with the shed in the back."

"You on your way?"

"Heading over. We're about halfway there."

"I'll meet you there." Rex ended the call and started his truck. He knew the house. The owner had just had some electrical work done the month before. It's where Rex met Colton Peters to ask him a few questions about the day Kelsey went missing.

He squealed his tires pulling out of the parking lot and secretly hoped that Ruth would hear it even though he didn't do it intentionally. He was about ten minutes away from his destination, but it felt like it took him a lifetime to get there. When he arrived, he wished it had taken longer.

SIX
MONTHS
EARLIER

Chapter II

The time has come. Casting shall commence.

Maris sat at the end of the counter, unconsciously dunking her tea bag in a mug of hot water. She watched June clean up the counters from the early morning breakfast rush. "I still think you should hire someone to at least wash the dishes for you. You deserve to give yourself a break. Hire one of the kids for summer break." Maris was a petite woman with a head full of gray, curly hair, and the oldest resident in town. Everyone in Dunmeyer agreed her spunky attitude is the reason she still seemed so young.

"I don't see the need. I've been doing this so long by myself, I think I'd get bored." She heard Maris sigh and she dropped the rag on the counter. "Okay. What if I promise to consider it, just for the summer?"

Maris dropped her teabag on the saucer. "Honey, I may be old, but I'm not dumb. If you don't want help, don't get help. I'll still get my daily cup of tea."

June's hearty laugh filled the nearly empty diner. "Leave it to you to have your priorities straight."

"Priorities? Ha. The only priorities I have left are making sure I put my pantyhose on the right way and remembering to use the bathroom before I pull them up. My tea is just an excuse to be social."

"You're the most social person I know, you don't need tea for that." She picked up the rag and moved to the two-person table closest to the counter, wiping toast crumbs into her hand.

"I know I don't need it, dear. Hence why I called it an excuse. You know better than anyone I could just buzz around town all day sticking my nose where it doesn't belong."

June smiled and nodded her head. She looked up when the bell above the door chimed to see Emily strut through. "Well, good morning, Sunshine. You're out and about early this morning." She noted that despite the early hour, Emily looked perfectly put together. Her silver hoops glistened in the sunlight streaming through the window, she had washed and dried her raven hair, and she had applied her makeup flawlessly.

She made her way to the counter and collapsed onto a stool two down from Maris. "I'm out of coffee."

'Say no more." June grabbed a mug off the shelf, filled it, and slid it across to Emily. June inherited the diner from her parents and it was her pride and joy, second only to her son. She did her best to keep it as authentic as she could, even keeping the original hours of five in the morning until seven at night. Sundays were the only exception when she worked half a day and didn't open until after church.

"You're a life saver." Emily took a big gulp of black coffee and didn't flinch at the temperature. June and Maris watched her in awe; nothing ever had any effect on her. It was an excellent quality to have for one who owned a bar, she had to be tough to own a business like that.

Maris couldn't stop her inquisitive mind and had no problem asking the questions that gave others pause. "This is an odd question, even coming from me, but what are you doing awake so early?" For years, she had gone to bed at nine and was up at four. For having such a social personality, Maris enjoyed the quiet before the rest of the town woke up.

Emily took the last sip of coffee and pushed the mug back across the counter to encourage June to refill it. "Oh, you know how it is. Parent first, sleep never."

"I've only heard rumors. Never did find a man who was lucky enough to be able to tame my sassy little butt." She winked at Emily. "You might not believe it now, but I was once the wildest one in this town."

June let out a laugh. "Maris, I think you still hold that honor."

"Agreed. I may look the part, but you've got me beat by miles. One of these days you'll have to teach me your ways."

Maris rested her elbow on the counter, her chin in her hand. She narrowed her eyes, scrutinizing Emily. "It won't be easy, but I think I can help you. If you're willing to learn, you could become my successor."

Emily finished her refill in three gulps, slid a five-dollar bill on the counter and stood to leave. She pushed open the door and called over her shoulder. "Challenge accepted."

Bill stood outside his grocery store filling an old, two-wheeled, wooden cart with apples when Emily arrived. His store was situated half-way down the town's main road. He inherited the business from his grandfather and kept it in its original condition. Linoleum covered the floor that had bowed and warped over the years. One register stood inside the door, placed atop a long, solid counter with chipped wood on the edges and no conveyor belt. Outside, a wooden walkway ran along the front at ground level, an awning stretched over it above the doorway. It didn't have any modern conveniences, but the locals still supported the business. "Good morning, Miss Emily. You're up early today."

Emily had always liked Bill despite him not being able to keep his eyes off her. He tried to hide it until the day she called him out on it. Since then, he didn't try anymore. It didn't bother her and her husband, Eli, thought it was funny that Bill liked her so much. "Morning, Bill. I didn't have much choice this morning, I ran out of coffee. There is no way I'd make it through my day without it."

"I understand. I need at least two cups myself before I can function properly. Anyway, I'll be in and out for the next few minutes so just yell when you're ready." Bill was thick around his middle with a full head of gray hair. His outfit of choice was always black sneakers, dark gray or brown slacks, and a dingy butcher's coat which aged him beyond his years.

"Thanks. I'll let you know."

Bill watched her walk away. Her jeans hugged every curve and it was one of his favorite scenes. Tattoos ran down the length of both her arms and in her tank top, he could see them covering her shoulders as well. The heavy rings on each hand could do real damage if the need arose. Her appearance perfectly matched her attitude and Bill spent countless hours fantasizing about what it would be like to be with her, wondering if that personality stayed with her in all situations. "Mmm. Shame she's taken," he muttered, shaking his head. Bill heard someone call his name from behind him and turned to see who it was. Suzanne had parked her pickup truck across the street and waved to him as she crossed.

"Hi, Bill."

"Oh hey, Suzanne." He shifted his eyes to look back inside the store, disappointed to see Emily had moved out of his line of sight. He busied himself rearranging his already perfect display of apples. "How are you doing today?"

"Doing well, thanks. Just need to pick up a few things. I won't be long."

Bill nodded. He knew she had already been busy working on the farm because of the fine layer of dirt and dust covering her faded Levis and sleeveless T-shirt she always wore with just the front tucked in. He didn't have to look to know she was leaving a trail of clumped, dried mud from her work boots in her wake. He liked Suzanne well enough but hated having to clean up after her. He filled a small display tree with bananas and went inside in time to see Suzanne and Emily approaching the counter together. The two didn't fit together. Emily, with her flawless makeup, clothes that accentuated all her features, and silky hair that Bill could all but feel brushing against his skin was in stark contrast with Suzanne's reddish-brown hair that fell in messy waves, the all-natural look of no make-up, and what he assumed were second-hand clothes. They all but ignored him, talking about their plans for lunch, as he rung up their purchases. He concluded there were five of them meeting that afternoon and he couldn't help the intense resentment he felt toward Emily at that moment. He had asked her to join him for lunch once, as friends, but she had politely declined. He didn't care that this was a group of women getting together. Jealousy still boiled inside him.

He barely acknowledged the other customers entering the store while he stood against the door frame, watching the women converse from across the street. When they left, he busied himself with the task of sweeping up the clumps of dirt on the floor. He'd asked Suzanne multiple times to kick off her boots before entering. When it was obvious she wasn't willing to comply, he invested in a long, rough mat to place in front of the door. It didn't help with her boots and only served with getting in his way while he was moving carts in and out. He rang up the purchases of his current patrons and put a sign on the door stating he would be back in ten minutes.

He was hopeful a freshly baked muffin and a hot coffee from the bakery would brighten his mood. Most days he held out until lunch before going to get his coffee. The bakery was only across the street and two buildings down, but the afternoon walk refreshed his energy that he needed to get through the rest of the day.

Sally greeted him as soon as he walked through the door. "You're early today. Tough day already?" A black hair net matted down her greying hair and her cheek had a streak of flour smeared across it; little specks dotted her nose.

"You could say that. I'm not only getting a coffee, I'm also buying a muffin." With a sigh, he sank into the chair closest to the counter.

A look of shock crossed Sally's face. "Oh. Would you like to talk about it? I'm all ears." She walked around the counter and pulled out the chair across the table from him before realizing she hadn't gotten his order yet. "What kind of muffin can I get for you?"

"Pistachio, please." He took a deep breath and the smell of freshly baked bread made his stomach rumble. His weakness wasn't the sweet, fruity smell of the muffins or pies, it was the aroma of the bread. He had to fight with himself every day to not bring home a loaf.

Sally set a plate on the table, along with a fork, and brought two cups of coffee over, settling into the seat across from him again. Knowing he wouldn't stay long, she put Bill's coffee in a to-go cup and her own in a mug. "So, what's raining on your parade today?"

Bill gave her a half-hearted smile. "I appreciate your willingness to listen, but I'll be fine. I'm just overthinking things as I always do. I think the walk over and getting out of the store for a few minutes was exactly what I needed." He shrugged before adding, "the muffin helps, too."

Disappointment washed over her. Sally loved gossip of any kind, even if it was just someone venting about their day. "Okay." She stood and grabbed her mug. "If you change your mind, you know where to find me." She tried to give him her best smile, but it lacked any genuine qualities. "Enjoy the rest of your day."

"Thank you. You as well." He slid a five and a couple singles onto the table, took his last bite of muffin, and walked slowly back to his store. He wasn't in a hurry and the sun was high enough now that he could feel the warmth from it. It was a welcome change from the cooler months before. Three customers stood outside the door waiting for him. He swore to himself before plastering on a fake smile and apologizing for his absence.

It was rare that all five ladies could find time to have lunch together. They tried to meet once a month when they didn't have their husbands or children around. It gave them a break from their daily routine, allowed them to gossip, complain about their husbands, and vent about any current frustrations. They all wanted friends to laugh and joke around with without anyone listening to their conversation or one of their children interrupting them. These lunches were their time away, a way to decompress, and enjoy each other's company. All of them had children who were either in their junior or senior year and none of them were prepared for them to go off to college and be on their own. They much preferred them at home, where they knew they were safe.

"So, are we talking about the kids today or are they off limits?" Suzanne was always inquisitive, but sometimes it was difficult to tell if she was being her usual, curious self or acting snarky.

"Off limits," Emily replied as she made her way to the table with the plates. "This is a lunch, not a weekend getaway. If we start talking about the children, we'll be here for days." Mumbles of agreement came from the other women as they claimed their seats at the dining table.

"Plus," Marilyn added, "talking about our husbands is much more entertaining."

"Really, Marilyn? Is that because you like to rub it in our faces that you never have anything bad to say about Rex?" Kimberley, stationed at her usual seat at the head of the table, reached out and grabbed a cucumber sandwich from the serving tray. She held it in her hand without taking a bite. "I mean, let's be fair. After all this time, we have to assume the only flaws he has are in the bedroom because he seems pretty perfect otherwise. So, spill it. Is he a one-minute man? Selfish? Prude? What is it? What's wrong with him?" She stopped and rolled her eyes to the ceiling as if looking for the answer there. "I've got it. He's routine. Every Sunday before church and that's it." Her eyebrows shot up and she stared at Marilyn, waiting for the answer.

The other three women had looks of amusement painted on their faces. They all wanted an answer as much as Kimberley did. Although a lot of people found Kimberley to be short-tempered, rude, and abrasive, the reality was that she was direct and didn't know how to filter the words that came out of her mouth. If a thought entered her head, it came out of her mouth with no concern for who was around. Often, she verbalized the things everyone was thinking but didn't have the courage to say.

A slanted smile crept across Marilyn's face. "If you really must know, we're awake until the wee hours of the morning three or four days a week. He always makes sure I'm satisfied," she held up two fingers in front of her, "twice per session, and despite what you may think, a bible is the furthest thing from what we keep in our nightstand drawers. Having a husband who carries handcuffs with him all day does have some benefits, you know."

"Well, shit," Emily blurted out. "You wanna switch?" Jaws dropped all around the table and she couldn't hide her smile. "Sorry, I didn't mean it *that* way. You all know I don't have any complaints there with Eli. He may be an asshole at times, but that's one time I know I can always count on him."

Suzanne stared into space, talking to no one in particular. Under her breath she muttered, "three or four times a week?"

June sighed and set her glass of tea on the table. "All right, guys. New subject."

"Mhm. Sandra Dee over here has had enough sex talk for the day." This time, Kimberley's comment had snark written all over it.

"I'm not a prude. I just don't think we need to talk about sex every time we get together."

Emily nodded. "You can be a little Sandra Dee-ish at times. But, I agree. New subject. Suzanne, how's the farm life treating you?"

"Same as always. Mostly shitty, but I can't argue with the fresh milk and eggs every day. I'm not looking forward to another hot, humid summer though. Summer days in the field are nothing but torture."

Marilyn couldn't help but laugh. "Just in case you've forgotten, we all have fresh eggs and milk every day. We get them from you."

"Well, then none of you should have any complaints either." She took the last bite of her macaroni salad. "Can we please talk about the kids? I have something I need to get reassurance about."

"No." The answer came in a form of surround sound from the other four sitting at the table.

Chapter III

I will prove to you that I am the master of manipulation.

Colton drove across town to find Frank, thankful to get away from the hardware store for a bit. The week had been quiet and he was growing bored and impatient with each passing minute. He spent the late morning and early afternoon hours outside in the fenced in area behind the store organizing the plants that arrived earlier in the morning. The gardening section was the most profitable for the small store and it was beginning to feel like spring had finally arrived. He was expecting large crowds over the weekend and had stocked up on all the essentials. This year, he had gone a step further and ordered in some garden gnomes, bird houses and baths, and even a few fountains hoping to earn a little extra income. His daughter, Beth-Ann, would be going into her senior year and then heading off to college the next year and he needed every penny he could get.

The firehouse was a small, red brick building with only one garage-style door, large enough to house the solitary truck the town needed. The building was old but well maintained. Colton found frank in the far corner, huddled in front of a small television playing a video game. "At least you're spending your time wisely." It didn't surprise Colton to see him wasting his time on such a trivial hobby, but he also didn't mind. Frank just turned twenty-five and hadn't found a woman to settle down with. He was known as being the most attractive man in Dunmeyer, regardless of the admirers' age. Despite the unsettling feeling it gave Colton to know that both his wife and his daughter found Frank attractive, the only thing that truly mattered was that Frank was professional and efficient when he needed to be.

Frank paused the game and looked over his shoulder. "Oh, hey. Yeah, I need to be able to kill time somehow. It's not like there's a whole lot of action around here. Last time I got a call was Tuesday night when your store alarm went off."

"That's actually one of the reasons I stopped by. I wanted to thank you again for that. I also wanted to see if you were still doing that fencing project for your yard. I need to put an order in before I leave today so if you need supplies, I'll make sure I get extra."

"Actually," he put his finger up to indicate he needed a minute and walked to the desk in the opposite corner. He flipped through some papers scattered along the desktop and raised a piece in the air. "I ran into you daughter the other day and she reminded me. I made a list of what I need." He handed it over and Colton looked it over.

"Can I take this?"

"Yeah. If you're ordering specifically for me, I'd like to go with the saddle brackets. I think they'll hold up best with the rain and mud in the spring season."

"I agree. The saddles are more expensive than the others. That okay?"

"Doesn't matter. A higher investment at the beginning could save a lot of money in the future if I don't have to fix it every few years."

"You got it."

"So," Frank changed the subject. "Is Beth-Ann leaving for college this summer?"

Colton's eyes narrowed and he hesitated before answering. "No. She still has another year left. Josh is graduating this year, but he's not planning on going to college. I've tried to convince him, but he wanted to stay here and take over the store."

"Mhm, Cyrus mentioned that, about Josh, I mean. If I were you, I would try harder to convince Josh to go and do your best to keep Beth-Ann home.

She's turning out to be quite...how do I put this?" He rolled his eyes to the ceiling while he concentrated. "Well, let's just say you should keep her away from all those city boys. I'm not much older than she is and..."

Colton put his finger up to stop him. "And you think those city boys are going to be worse than the good ole country boys we have right here in town?" Frank opened his mouth to speak and Colton interrupted before he had a chance. "Don't say another word." He turned to leave, heat radiating from every part of his body. As he neared the entrance he turned back, holding up the piece of paper with Frank's order on it. "I'll get this stuff ordered for you. And if you know what's good for you, you'll stay away from my daughter." The last words came out as a growl between clenched teeth. Colton had no trouble talking man to man, but he took it personally when someone was talking about his daughter in a disrespectful manner.

He slammed the door of his truck and spun his tires as he raced away from the firehouse. He knew his daughter was beautiful. He worried every day about what it would be like once she left for college. But Frank, even as young as he is, should know not to say anything about another man's daughter to his face.

When he got back to the hardware store, he placed the order for the next month, including the fencing supplies Frank requested, and told Cyrus he was leaving for the rest of the day. Cyrus tried to ask if he was okay, but Colton ignored him and walked out the door. Frank and Cyrus grew up together and had been best friends since they were about five years old. He didn't want to involve Cyrus and he knew Frank would tell him everything sooner rather than later.

Beth-Ann Peters sat at the high-topped bar in the pharmacy. Her root beer float sat untouched and clumps of thick, sticky foam dripped over the rim of the glass. Her textbook and spiral notebook were both open in front of her, a blank, lined page staring back at her. She dropped her pen on the notebook purposely for dramatic effect. "Ugh. Chemistry is the worst. Like, why do I even need to learn this? I'm literally never going to use this, ever."

"I know. All it does is stress me out. I've been sitting here for twenty minutes, just staring at the first question and I don't even know what the question actually is." Kelsey took a bite of her ice cream and dropped the spoon back in the bowl. "Who ever uses this stuff in real life?"

Jake stood in the far corner, back to the girls, filling out paperwork. He laughed before turning to face them. "Actually, ladies, I use this stuff in real life. You can't become a pharmacist without knowing how certain chemicals react with other chemicals. It could literally be the difference between life and death."

Beth-Ann stared at him. "Okay, but...I'm not going to be a pharmacist, no offense. So, what is the point of me learning it?" She used her finger to swipe some fizz off the side of her glass and licked it off.

"No offense taken. And while I don't have a good answer to give you for that exact question, I can tell you some people just have a knack for it. You'll never know if you're good at something, or if you'll like it, unless you give it a try. Do you two think I might be able to help you out with your homework?"

The pharmacy was old. It still had all the original display cases with filigree carvings on the side and counters from back when they built things to last. If he had the items in this store appraised, Jake guessed they would be more valuable than anything found in any of the other buildings in town. When he took over the shop many years ago, some local residents suggested updating the place to make it more modern. Jake wouldn't entertain the idea. Between the display cases, the ice cream bar, and the burnt orange, linoleum flooring, the building had personality to it, something you couldn't find in the modernized structures.

Kelsey was stirring her ice cream into a bowl of soup. "I could definitely use the help if you're willing. Seriously, just reading the first question makes my brain hurt, never mind trying to figure out the answer."

Teenagers had been coming to the pharmacy after school for years. Usually, they got a drink or a snack and sat at the counter to work on their homework until it was time to go home for dinner. Jake never minded, even when they didn't purchase anything. The children always minded well and never caused any trouble.

Jake helped Beth-Ann and Kelsey with the first three questions and when he was confident they had a decent understanding of how to solve the equations, he left them to their own devices and went back to his paperwork. He knew from personal experience most of these would never leave town for long and they really wouldn't need to know Chemistry. The teenagers may leave for college or move out to see what life in a big city was like, but after a few years, they would return home. They almost always did. Small town living creates a nostalgia that they wouldn't be able to find anywhere else.

Like Maris, everyone saw Jake as the grandfather of the town even though he was only sixty-two. He was friendly, personable, and genuine. He was well-liked by everyone in town. Years ago, he was one of those teenagers that left, thinking he would never return. He went to college, got his degree, and realized how much he missed home. He moved back to Dunmeyer, did his internship, and took over the pharmacy a year later.

Jake was just shy of being six feet tall. He had grey hair combed to one side and oiled down. He always wore black, woven pants and under his white pharmacist's coat, wore either a pressed, white tee shirt or a dark blue sweater. He always looked presentable, but his wardrobe held no variety.

Bobby walked up to the pharmacy and pressed his face against the front window. He could see Kelsey sitting at the bar, leaning over her notebook, chewing the cap of her pen. That was a quirk she had when she was trying to concentrate and Bobby knew never to interrupt her pen chewing. She had her light brown hair pulled into a loose ponytail and Bobby loved the way her hair spiraled at the ends. Every time they curled up together, he found himself winding the spirals around his fingers. They didn't have any classes together on Fridays and Bobby couldn't wait to go inside to see her, but Beth-Ann was also there. He still couldn't believe they stayed such close friends. Beth-Ann and Bobby dated over the last summer and made it until just after the new year. Two weeks after they broke up, he started dating Kelsey. Beth-Ann and Kelsey didn't speak to each other for a month and then, almost overnight, the became best friends again and thought nothing of it. Even though it didn't bother them, it still made Bobby uncomfortable being around both of them. He never let that feeling stop him, he just preferred their alone time. Bobby and Beth-Ann still got along, they didn't have a bad break-up and they had been friends for years. He pulled the door wide, strode up to Kelsey and wrapped his arms around her. "Hey, babe." He landed a kiss on the top of her head and pulled up a chair next to her. "What are you working on?" He grabbed her spoon and took a huge bite of her half liquid ice cream.

Kelsey looked at him like she was ready to bite his face off but slowly smiled instead. "I finally figured out how to do this chemistry homework, thanks to Jake, so I'm finishing it up now. Do you mind if I take a few minutes for this last question?"

"Not at all, work away." He leaned forward and waved to Beth-Ann. "Hello to you as well."

"Hey, Bobby." She barely diverted her eyes to look at him. "How are you?"

"Same as I was about two hours ago when I last saw you. It's Fri-day, which means we get to par-tay." The biggest grin stretched across his face. Bobby loved Friday nights. Every week, winter, summer, it didn't matter to him, he had to build the biggest bonfire anyone had ever seen. It was his personal mission to build one bigger and better every week. Most of the people who went to the parties were impressed that he hadn't caught the woods on fire yet. He would never purposely do it, he contained his fires well, he just always wanted to outdo himself. As a teenager in a small town like Dunmeyer, there wasn't much to do so they made their fun. In the summer, they took trips to neighboring towns to go see a movie or visit an amusement park, but the rest of the year they were stuck. It was harder a few years ago when no one in their group had a license. Rex allowed the teens to drive around town without giving them a hard time, but none of them would ever have left the town limits.

Bobby and a few friends had beat up old trucks they bought for a couple hundred dollars each that they used to cruise around in. They had open fields, no longer used for anything, so they often took their trucks out and went joyriding and mudding through the fields, especially during spring when it was rainy. None of them would be able to count the number of times their trucks had gotten stuck and they had to go back a day or two later, after things dried out, to retrieve their vehicle. None of their parents said anything to them, as they weren't hurting anyone, although a few residents said something about allowing the children to participate in such "devilish activities." Their parents laughed it off and relayed the conversation to the teens in a humorous fashion.

They were simply kids being kids. Although they knew they would never admit it, all the kids assumed their parents did the same sort of thing when they were their age. When their parents were growing up, they didn't have the internet or cell phones readily available, so they knew they had to find a way to cause trouble. Not one single adult in Dunmeyer was completely wholesome or innocent, no matter how much they tried to play it off. Even Maris had a wild streak to her.

Bobby jumped when the bell on the door chimed. He looked over and saw Roy Carlson walk in. He stood and put his hand in the air. "What's up?" They grabbed hands and gave a quick, one-armed hug, bumping chests in the process. "I didn't know you were coming around this afternoon."

"Yeah, I figured I'd stop in and say 'hi' before I went home for dinner. We still lightin' it up later?"

"You know we are."

Roy walked sideways, away from Bobby, and leaned down to give Beth-Ann a kiss. "Hi, doll." He kept his eyes toward the counter, away from Bobby, but stiffened knowing Bobby may express some kind of negative reaction. The two boys had been best friends since they were toddlers. They did everything together. The one thing they had never done was date one of the other's exes. To his surprise, Bobby didn't say anything or even move.

"Hi. I'll be ready to go in just a few minutes." Beth-Ann smiled at him as wide as she could.

Bobby slipped his arm around Kelsey's waist and turned to stare out the window. He knew he couldn't say anything. He broke up with Beth-Ann and started dating her best friend. It felt different now that it was happening to him. His best friend was dating his ex. He felt the anger rise inside him, felt disrespected that neither of them took the time to tell him. Roy could have told him at any time rather than letting him find out like this. At least he and Kelsey kept it under wraps until she got up the courage to tell Beth-Ann. Kelsey seemed unaffected by what had just happened and Bobby slowly slid his hand across her back, releasing his hold on her. He was angry about the situation, but would be even angrier if Kelsey knew and chose not to tell him. She was supposed to tell him everything, that was how relationships were supposed to work. Maybe she assumed he already knew and didn't want to bring up a potentially touchy subject even though he shouldn't care about Beth-Ann in that way anymore. For Bobby, it was less about Beth-Ann and more about his relationship with Roy. He thought better of his friend and felt he deserved better from him. He tapped his foot on the bar of the stool it was resting on, trying not to say anything. He didn't want to create a scene in the middle of the pharmacy. He would see all of them later and would be able to confront each one of them. He planned to do just that.

He didn't say a word to anyone while the girls were finishing their homework. When Kelsey finished, he stood and gave a half-hearted wave to Beth-Ann and Roy. They both said their goodbyes to him and Kelsey and said they would see them later. Bobby had planned to give Kelsey a ride home, but was hoping for a little affection before dropping her off. He was no longer in the mood and didn't speak to her until she spoke first when they were halfway to her house.

"You haven't said anything since before we left. Are you okay?" She ran her hand across the top of his leg, gripping his inner thigh lightly.

He glanced over at her and could see the concern in her eyes. Maybe she didn't understand. "Yeah, I'm fine. I know I don't have the right to say anything, but I wish someone would have said something about Roy and Beth-Ann. He's supposed to be my best friend, you know?"

Kelsey sat back against the seat, hung her head, and pinched her lips together. His being upset about this made her feel like a bad guy, not because she didn't tell him, she only found out early that afternoon, but because she was Beth-Ann's best friend and she had done the same thing to her. She didn't think Bobby understood that part. Either that, or he was talking out of anger and hurt and not thinking about things as they really were.

He glanced at her again and saw both the shock and hurt on her face. He reached over and grabbed her loosely fisted hand. "I'm sorry, Kels. I didn't think about what I was saying. All I meant was that, as my best friend, Roy should have said something to me before I found out like this. He should have told me the exact same way you told Beth-Ann. I guess...I don't know. I guess I just thought better of him. I figured he had enough trust in me and respect for me to tell me, guy to guy."

Kelsey ran her fingers along the edge of the seat where exposed foam showed through the vinyl split from age and abuse. She felt mildly better after his explanation. She knew he was upset, she didn't blame him. She just wished he talked to Roy instead of putting her in the middle. Roy could give him a real explanation then he could vent to her all he wanted. She was already dreading the conversation she would have with Beth-Ann. She knew as soon as Roy and Bobby talked, she would have to listen to Beth-Ann complain about how unfair Bobby was being. To Beth-Ann, it didn't matter what it was about or who was at fault, she would always blame the person who was the least connected to her. Kelsey was thankful when they pulled into her driveway and she leaned over and gave Bobby a kiss. "Pick me up at seven?"

"You got it."

Bobby didn't bother to go home for dinner. He spent the next two and a half hours driving aimlessly around town. Before picking Kelsey back up, he stopped for a few minutes to set up the firepit. He took out some frustration by breaking branches and chopping up a few logs for firewood. He couldn't decide if he was mad or upset but swinging an ax made him feel better. Aside from being in one of his favorite places, he enjoyed knowing that spring had arrived. It was still light outside when he got back in his truck and that meant summer would be here before he knew it.

Sitting in Kelsey's driveway, he stared at her when she walked out the front door. She changed into a pair of skinny blue jeans, brown ankle boots, and a blue and orange flannel shirt that she tied at her waist. He leaned out his window and waved to her father while she jumped in the truck. She slid across the seat and kissed him like she had only a couple of hours before.

They pulled into the makeshift parking lot just in time to see Kelsey's brother, Clint, flick a lighter and lean down to start the fire. Bobby slammed his truck into park, threw his door open, and stood up so he was hanging out the door. "Back off my bonfire, bitch!"

Quite a large group had already gathered around. They turned when they heard his voice and all at once yelled out, "Bobby."

Clint stood and flashed him the widest grin. "Hey, buddy. I was just going to get it started for you." As usual, he wore jeans, a white t-shirt, and his baseball cap sat backwards on his head.

Bobby jumped out of the truck. "And I'm just going to start breaking your fingers if you touch my fire pit again." They grabbed hands, pulled into each other, and each gave the other one pat on the back.

Kelsey had already gotten out of the truck and joined a group of friends. She knew it was unlikely she would see Bobby again until it was time to go home. Party nights were hard for her. She loved spending time with her friends just as much as she loved spending time with Bobby, but aside from an occasional quick kiss, he all but forgot she existed when his friends were around.

Roy and Beth-Ann didn't show up until almost an hour later. Roy walked over to join the guys at the fire and Beth-Ann made her way over to Kelsey. "Hey. I thought you two forgot how to get here."

Beth-Ann shook her head. "No. We would have been here sooner. We got into an argument about Bobby."

"Bobby? Why?"

"Because. I told you this afternoon about Roy and I because I thought he told Bobby. He didn't. I knew as soon as I saw Bobby's reaction in the pharmacy."

Kelsey scrunched her face. "I don't know if I'm the right person to talk to about this. I mean, I was in the same position a few months ago."

"Yeah, you were. But you and Bobby kept it hidden until you told me. You didn't walk up and kiss him unexpectedly. Roy should have said something."

Kelsey noticed about thirty minutes later that Bobby's truck was missing. He hadn't told her he was leaving, but she assumed and hoped he was coming back. She saw him pull back into the lot right after retrieving another drink. Roy got out of the passenger side and slammed the door on his exit. Now, at least, Kelsey knew where they had been, grateful they hadn't tried to drag her into it. She finished the conversation she was having and broke away to find Bobby. She wanted to make sure he was okay. She couldn't see him right away but heard the commotion from the far end of the parking lot. The volume got the attention of quite a few people and they all made their way toward the noise.

Beth-Ann and Bobby were in a heated discussion. She was trying to blame him for something, he was telling her everything was her fault. Aside from Roy and Kelsey, no one else had any idea what they were talking about. Roy ran up and got between the two as soon as he realized what was going on. He didn't say a word to either of them. He gently grabbed the back of Beth-Ann's arm and pulled her toward his truck, leaving Bobby standing by himself. Roy spun his tires in the dirt as he backed up and did the same when he put his truck in drive. Kelsey went directly to Bobby to make sure he was okay. He turned his head away from her and she couldn't tell if it was out of shame or anger. He turned back, ran his hand over her lower arm to let her know it wasn't personal against her, and walked away.

Bobby spent the next two hours sitting off to the side, not speaking to anyone. Kelsey didn't try to approach him. She knew if he wanted to talk to her, he would come find her. She did her best to enjoy her evening, taking her parents' advice on not letting other people get her down. It was hard watching him Bobby so upset, he was normally playful and fun-loving. When he finally joined her, he sat quietly beside her, wrapped his arm around her waist, and leaned his head on her shoulder. She reciprocated by leaning her head against his. Neither of them spoke, they didn't have to. They hadn't been together long, but they had a connection. Kelsey knew he was telling her he was sorry and she was telling him she understood. The party had died down to only a few stragglers and the fire had died down as well. After all the fuss at the beginning of the evening, Bobby didn't get to enjoy what he always tried so hard for.

"Want to help me put the fire out? Then I'll bring you home."

Kelsey nodded. It was nearing midnight and she hadn't realized until then how tired she was. She was ready for their summer break. She took the gallon jugs of water Bobby handed her and began splashing them on what was remaining of the fire. It took ten gallons before Bobby decided it was safe to leave.

They rode to Kelsey's house in silence again. She had her window all the way down, enjoying the feel of the cool night air against her face. She loved this time of year when everything smelled fresh and new. Her body relaxed with the breeze and Bobby slid his hand over her thigh, making her feel even better. All her worries about Bobby and Beth-Ann disappeared the moment he touched her. When they pulled up to her house, Bobby leaned in and gave her a slow, passionate kiss. This was what she waited all night for. His kiss said more than any words could. "Will you call me tomorrow? Maybe we can hang out for a little bit?"

"You know I will. Have a good night." Kelsey opened the front door of her house just in time to not break curfew. Her parents weren't strict about many things, but the curfew was the one rule they wouldn't budge on. They always claimed they couldn't sleep until they knew all the kids were home, but she didn't buy it since they always seemed to be fast asleep when she got home. Knowing it wouldn't do any good, she always tried to push back and ask for an extension. It wouldn't matter much seeing as it was more of a town curfew and all her friends also had to be home by midnight. Still, she was determined.

After waking her mother and letting her know she arrived safely, she lay on the top of her bed and promptly fell asleep. She didn't take the time to crawl under the covers or change into pajamas. Even her boots were still on her feet when her mother came and woke her up around ten in the morning. She was still exhausted and felt like she hadn't slept at all.

For the next half hour, she tossed and turned. The phone downstairs rang non-stop. She could hear her mother answer but only got bits and pieces of what her mother was saying. She heard the low rumble of her parents deep in conversation and she pulled her pillow over her head to try to drown out the noise.

She heard the footsteps on the stairs and she grumbled. She knew her mother wouldn't let her sleep any longer. Her door burst open without so much as a knock and her mother walked in.

"Kelsey. Wake up right now." She sounded panicked. "Where's Beth-Ann? Is she here?"

Kelsey grunted her reply. "No. She went home last night."

"No, sweetheart. She didn't."

Chapter IV

Jealousy is an ugly thing. If you're not careful, it will consume you.

There were a few years between us; my sister, three years my junior, the obvious favorite. As far back as I can remember, our mother treated her so differently, adored her in every way. Why wouldn't she? My sister was beautiful, intelligent, friendly. I possessed none of those qualities. At the age of about five, she found a love for puppets. Not of the hand-sock variety or paper cutout kind, but expensive, intricately designed puppets. Marionettes. She found herself taken by their fluid, human movements, their exquisite style of dress.

Our mother, being a single parent, often left us to care for ourselves. Our dinners consisted of cold cereal and toast, an occasional sandwich when we were lucky. She began working longer hours, coming home only after we had settled for bed. I remember the shock of her appearing early one night, two wrapped presents in her hands. I can still picture the shiny, polka dot paper, the large yellow bows melting over the sides. My sister and I looked at each other, our eyes wide with excitement, hearts racing in anticipation. We never received gifts. Even Christmas and birthdays, built up by teachers and friends, brought about disappointment when we opened well-worn shoes or not-so-gently used toys. Our mother set the boxes on the table and motioned my sister over, pushing the taller package toward her. My sister tore the paper away in one swipe, clawing at the top of the box to reveal its contents. Squealing in delight, she reached in to pull the object out. A marionette. Perfect facial features, rosy cheeks on smooth, porcelain skin, wearing a royal blue, velvet dress trimmed with black lace. She ran her fingertips along the fabric, smiling at the sensation.

I stepped forward to claim the second box and the heel of my mother's palm met my forehead, holding me in place while she encouraged my sister to open the other box. She took time with this one, peeling back the paper at its seams. Removing the top, she used both hands to reveal a dress, her size, perfectly matching that of her toy. I watched with eyes clouded with tears as she changed into her new dress, my mother only removing her hand from my forehead to help her with the zipper. I stood in the same spot for hours, long after they walked away.

No gift box with shiny polka dots or a big yellow bow ever appeared for me.

This type of event became routine. Every few months I watched my sister delight in opening a new doll, trying on a new dress, while my mind slowly withdrew from it all. I tried to join in. I asked to play with the puppets. My sister screamed; the back of my mother's hand left an aching red mark on my cheek. My mother forbade me from touching the dolls, telling me over and over I would be too rough, I would ruin their dresses, I would mark their faces.

Two years passed and I finally gave in, I asked for my own puppet. They both laughed and ridiculed me, my mother reminded me I wasn't gentle or delicate like my sister; I didn't hold the kind of talent, patience, or determination that make up the necessary skill set to become a master puppeteer. But I never wanted a stupid puppet. I didn't want to learn to control them, to manipulate them, to make them move on my command. I wanted the attention, the presents, the adoration from my mother. I wanted to feel wanted.

At twelve years of age, I had gone from being a shy, lonely child, to a troublemaker looking for attention wherever I could find it. I tried to find a hobby, something to make my mother proud. I was terrible at writing; I could barely draw a cloud. I couldn't sing or dance or even hit a ball. My grades were poor, my attendance was lacking. I became messy, lazy, and a terrible, habitual liar. I turned into a bully, making other kids cry. My school suspended me, gave me detention, they even asked my mother to change my school. She refused. When another parent called my mother, she slapped me around and I went and did it all again the next day. Good, bad, and no matter how brief, I enjoyed the attention.

I used to watch my sister from afar, made up in her velvet or silken dresses, her lips shiny with gloss, rouge on the apples of her cheeks. She sat in the corner and moved the marionette's strings meticulously back and forth. She did have a talent. Within months of receiving her first gift, she learned to control two at once. It was mesmerizing. Not the puppets themselves, but the way she could make them dance. She rolled her wrists and twisted her fingers, used different combinations to create rhythmic movements. Her hand gestures were elegant, almost imperceptible. But dance her puppets did, with energy and pizazz.

Suzanne sat on the edge of Kelsey's bed, a pleading look in her eyes. "Sit up and talk to me. Where did Beth-Ann go last night?"

"I don't know," Kelsey whined. "She left the party with Roy because she got into an argument with Bobby. Maybe she went back to his house."

"She didn't. Her mother already tried there."

Kelsey stared at her, trying to fight the brain fog and comprehend what her mother was trying to tell her. "Why does it matter?"

"Kelsey," Suzanne snapped. "I know you're still half asleep, but your best friend is missing. Do you understand that? No one has seen her since last night. I need you to wake up and tell me what happened."

That knowledge helped to wake her up. "I did tell you. Her and Bobby got into an argument at the party. They were yelling at each other. Roy got between them and walked Beth-Ann to his truck and they left. That's the last time I saw either one of them."

"How did you get home last night?"

"Bobby drove me home. He was upset because he found out yesterday afternoon that Beth-Ann and Roy are dating." She rubbed the sleep from her eyes. "That's why they were arguing."

Suzanne tried and failed to stifle a laugh. "Beth-Ann and Bobby's best friend are dating? And Bobby is dating her best friend after they dated each other? You kids are too much. You are all way too young to be in such a position. How weird is that for all of you?" She shook her head in amusement.

"Mom, seriously? I don't think we really need to worry about that right now. Besides, it's not like any of us meant to do it. It just happened."

"You're right and I'm sorry. Get up, change your clothes, and go call Beth-Ann's mom. She's waiting for your call. She's worried sick. Just tell her all the stuff you just told me. Maybe something you have to say can help her find out where she is."

"Okay. I'll be down in a couple minutes." Kelsey watched her mother walk out the door and took a deep breath. *Where could Beth-Ann be?* She assumed Roy would have taken her straight home since neither of them seemed to be in a socializing mood.

Kelsey changed into a clean pair of jeans and a plaid, buttoned shirt and pulled her hair back into a loose ponytail. Half-way down the stairs, she heard the house phone ring and her mother answered it. When she walked around the corner, her mother handed her the phone.

"It's Bobby. Make it quick so you can call Kimberley."

"I will." She took the phone and put it to her ear. "Good morning."

"Hey, babe. Beth-Ann is missing."

"I know. My mom just woke me to tell me. You don't have any idea where she is?"

"Not at all. I haven't seen her since we argued last night."

"That's the same time I saw her. She got in Roy's truck and left. I don't suppose you've talked to him yet?" She was hesitant to ask but needed to know.

"Actually, I did. We put everything aside. This is way more important than out stupid argument."

"He doesn't know where she is? He was the last one with her."

"No. He said they started arguing again and he left her at the end of her road when she demanded to be let out."

"Her's is the first house. What did she do, fall through her driveway?" She momentarily forgot about the seriousness of the situation. Her mother glanced at her and then tapped her wrist to tell her to hurry up her conversation. "I'm sorry. That was inappropriate. Um, I have to go. I have to call Beth-Ann's mom to see what I can do to help."

"Okay. I have a couple of things to do, but I'm going to come pick you up. I'll be there in about an hour."

"Sounds good. Bye." She ended the call and laid the phone on the table. "This is a nightmare." She wasn't speaking to anyone in particular. She picked the phone back up, possibly one of only twenty landlines left in the state, and called Kimberley.

Suzanne stood with the ear to the phone so she could listen to the conversation as well. Usually, Kelsey would be annoyed, but today she understood the need to listen in. She told Kimberley Bobby would be picking her up soon and she would have him drive her over to the house so they could talk in person. Kelsey felt awful. Aside from her best friend missing, she could hear how distraught her mother was, how useless she felt at that moment. Kelsey wanted to tell her not to worry and that everything would be okay, but she knew those words wouldn't help to make either of them feel better. Nothing would make them feel better except Beth-Ann coming home.

Kelsey sat at the kitchen table while she waited for Bobby to arrive. Beth-Ann wasn't the type of person to run away or hide from anything, even if she was upset. As much as Kelsey wanted the truth, she knew her best friend better than that and she knew in her heart that something was seriously wrong. If she did disappear, and what Roy was saying was true, that meant she went missing within a few feet of the end of her driveway. *Did Roy really drop her off there? What could possibly have gone wrong in such a short distance? What time did he actually drop her off?* Beth-Ann and Roy weren't at the party long. More than anything, she wanted to speak to Roy, find out exactly what happened between the two of them. She had so many questions running through her mind she couldn't keep them all straight. She couldn't imagine how Beth-Ann's parents must be feeling. She didn't understand how they could be keeping themselves together so well.

Suzanne made a bowl of oatmeal, poured a glass of juice, and set them both in front of Kelsey. Kelsey didn't feel like eating. She ate a couple bites before pushing the bowl away. Just the smell of it made her feel sick.

"I know you're not feeling very well at the moment, but you need to get something in your system. At least drink the juice." She flashed Kelsey a sympathetic smile, but in her head, she felt like she could explode at any minute. She wanted to hug Kelsey, pull her tight, and never let go. She didn't want her out of her sight, she didn't want her to leave the house, she didn't want Bobby bringing her to Beth-Ann's. She watched too many movies and saw too many news reports of children going missing. She only thought they were terrible until something like that happened so close to home. She wanted to be logical and remain calm knowing it had only been a few hours. Beth-Ann could simply be hiding out at a friend's house. From the information gathered so far, she had a rough day, for a teenager at least. But Suzanne's gut told her Beth-Ann wasn't hiding out. She saw Beth-Ann as a second daughter and she was putting a lot of energy into keeping her emotions together for Kelsey's sake. She knew the moment her daughter walked out the door she would break down.

Bobby knocked on the door gently before letting himself in. Usually, he sat in his truck and texted Kelsey to let her know he was there. Today, he felt it would be inappropriate to do that. In a small town like Dunmeyer, everyone knew each other and he had been coming to Kelsey's house for years. It wasn't a big deal for him to walk in without knocking or to show up unannounced. Her parents were always welcoming. "Hey, babe." He kissed the top of Kelsey's head and rested his hand on her back. "How are you doing?" It was a weird question to ask. He knew she felt terrible. He felt terrible. In his head, he thought Beth-Ann might appear after a few hours, completely unaware that people thought she was missing.

"I'm not really sure to be honest with you. But I do need to go to Beth-Ann's house to talk to her parents. I told her I would ask you to drive me over. I hope you don't mind."

She sounded distraught and Bobby wanted to gather her in his arms. He didn't. "Of course I don't mind. Let's head over now."

It was a ten-minute trip from Kelsey's house to Beth-Ann's, quicker to walk. The ride was silent until Bobby glanced over and saw Kelsey's eyes welling up with tears. "Hey. It's going to be okay, Kels. What I was thinking is that, since she'd been arguing with a couple of us yesterday, that she went to spend the night at someone else's house. She may be sitting at somebody's kitchen table right now and doesn't even know we think she's missing. This whole thing may be a complete misunderstanding." He knew his words wouldn't completely help, but he hoped they might put her mind at ease.

Kelsey shook her head. "I don't feel like she is. She's my best friend. I don't think she's ever gone anywhere without telling her parents first. Plus, it's almost noon. She would have at least called them by now." She turned her head and looked out the window, afraid she would break down in tears. She took a few slow, deep breaths to calm herself. It wouldn't do any good if she lost control and started crying in front of Kimberley.

When they pulled into the driveway, they saw Rex's truck parked near the front door. Kelsey turned her head to look at Bobby. "He thinks it's serious enough to come out."

"Oh, Kels. He has to come out for any reports he gets. Plus, it's a small town and nothing ever happens here. He probably has nothing else to do with his time. Let's go inside, we'll tell them what we know, and then we'll find out what they have to say. Okay?" His eyes pleaded with her.

"Okay." She dropped her head, opened the passenger door, and stepped out. She knocked on the front door quietly before opening it and calling out to let them know she was there. She heard Beth-Ann's father yell from the kitchen.

"In here, sweetie. Come on in."

They were all sitting around the kitchen table, Kimberley with her hands folded on the top. Rex had his notebook out and was busy jotting down notes. They all greeted both her and Bobby.

"I'm glad you're both here. Find a seat and I'll talk to you in a few minutes." Rex went back to writing in his notebook.

Kelsey had practically grown up in this house. It was always like a second home to her. Her older brother Clint and Beth-Ann's older brother Josh were the same age. She and Beth-Ann were the same age and their two younger siblings, Jimmy and Oscar, were the same. She had never felt more uncomfortable in this house than she did now. She tried sitting on one of the stools that lined the kitchen island, but kept squirming, trying to get comfortable. Bobby stood beside her and rested his hand on her thigh, trying to calm her. Aside from being Beth-Ann's ex, he had also never been so uncomfortable. It was awful for both of them to watch Beth-Ann's parents with such morose looks on their faces. Even Oscar was sitting quietly with watery eyes. They all looked like they had lost her for good.

When Rex finally turned to them, they were both on the verge of crying. "I wasn't going to talk to you two until later, I was planning to speak to Roy first, but this works. My understanding is that you were both together all day yesterday. Is that correct?"

"Yes," Bobby answered.

"No," Kelsey replied at the same time. They looked at each other with their lips curled in confusion.

"Kelsey, since you said 'no,' tell me your version of events from yesterday starting from when you left school." He poised his pen over his notebook, ready to capture everything she said.

"Okay. Um, we left school, Beth-Ann and I, and went to the pharmacy for ice cream and to do our homework. We were there for about two hours. Jake helped us with our chemistry homework. Bobby showed up about twenty minutes before him and I left. Roy got there about five minutes before we left. Bobby brought me home so I could have dinner and then he picked me up at home at seven so we could go to the fire." She felt as though all of her nerves were on fire. She talked fast and words were spilling out before she could stop them, like she was guilty of something.

"And where were Beth-Ann and Roy at that point?"

Kelsey shrugged. "I don't know. They were still at the pharmacy when we left." She paused to remember where she left off. "We got to the fire and there were a few people already there. The two of us split up and I went to hang out with the girls and Bobby stayed back with the guys. Beth-Ann got there about an hour later. She was upset because she had been fighting with Roy." She saw the questioning look on Rex's face. "Beth-An and Roy started dating a few weeks ago. I'm sure you know Bobby and Roy are best friends. Bobby is Beth-Ann's ex. Anyway, she thought Roy had told Bobby about them, but he didn't. Bobby just found out yesterday when he saw Roy lean down and kiss Beth-Ann at the pharmacy. So, they got into an argument about that. While we were at the fire, Bobby and Roy went out for a drive and even though I didn't get any details, I could see that they were both mad when they got back. At some point, I don't know what time, Bobby and Beth-Ann got into a heated discussion and Roy walked between the two of them and brought Beth-Ann over to his truck and they left. That was the last time either of us saw them. We assumed they had both gone home." This was the third time in less than three hours that she had told the exact same recollection of events and she was already tired of hearing it.

Rex nodded along as he recorded her chain of events. "Bobby? Anything to add?"

"No. that's pretty much what happened."

"Pretty much?"

"Well, yeah. I mean, it is what happened. But with Roy and I, it was...well, he thought I should have been cooler about him and Beth-Ann since I basically did the same thing. You know, because I started dating my ex's best friend. I guess it's different when you're on the other side of things." He sighed. "And the argument I had with Beth-Ann? It was stupid. She was trying to tell me I shouldn't be upset with Roy because I had done the same thing with her and Kelsey. I knew it was wrong to be mad, so I tried to blame it on her for not telling me. I didn't have a better argument than that. I just...now I..." He dropped his shoulders as his voice caught in his throat.

They all felt that pull inside. Every person present was only as strong as the next person in the room. They all felt they needed to stay strong for everyone else. They all felt the energy in the room that was making them anxious. Even Rex, who should have had the easiest time, given his line of work, was forcing his calm façade.

Rex was born and raised in Dunmeyer. When he graduated from the academy, he worked as an officer in a large city, becoming a detective within a few short years. Having been assigned to missing persons, one of the first things he was taught was to not let the cases get to him. He was supposed to pretend he didn't have any emotions; he wasn't supposed to get close to the victims or their families. He couldn't have any personal connection to them. It was much easier to do when he didn't know the people. Here, he knew Kimberley and Colton, he knew their children. Beth-Ann was friends with his own daughter.

"All right. I think that's it for now. I may reach out to each of you if I find any questions that I need to follow up on. He stood and secured his notebook in his pocket, still trying to put together the exact scenario of the four teenagers all dating one another. "Kimberley, you have that list of people to call?"

"I do. Right here." She raised the printout from the school that had contact information for all Beth-Ann's classmates.

"Great. Give me a call if you find anything you think may be helpful."

"I will. Thank you."

"Thank you all for answering my questions. I'm heading over to see Roy now and I'll be in touch."

Colton stood and walked Rex out to his truck. "Listen, sheriff? I need you to do me a favor."

Rex nodded. "I'm going to do everything I can to bring Beth-Ann home safely." The corners of his lips curled in a sympathetic smile.

"No, I know you will. But it's more than that. You know I've known Frank a long time, really since he was born." He fidgeted with the hem of his shirt, stalling for time. "Yesterday, I was pretty heated when I left the firehouse after I went to see him. I've had some time to think about it and I don't think he meant anything by it, but...well, he made a remark about Beth-Ann growing up and how I needed to keep an eye on her, referring to her looks. I'd appreciate it if you'd go talk to him."

"Of course. I'll add that to my list along with the Carlson's place."

"Thanks. And, I didn't say anything to Kimberley and I know Josh would beat him mercilessly if he knew what he said, so..."

"I understand. I'll let you know what I find out." Rex dropped his hand on Colton's shoulder and squeezed, letting him know he understood before getting into his truck without another word.

Chapter V

The stage is set. Rehearsals shall begin.

I open my eyes and all I can see is black. Instinctively, I try to stretch my limbs and a burning sensation rips through my shoulders. Panic sets in as I realize my captor shackled my arms to the wall with just enough slack so my toes can barely scrape the floor. I shiver and the concrete wall behind me tears at my skin. My head is foggy. It's takes me a moment to notice he left me in just my undergarments.

I fell asleep a few times before he came into the room, but every time my body went limp, the ropes tore at my wrists and threatened to dislocate my shoulders. I fought to stay awake against the resistance behind my eyes and the exhaustion running through my limbs. I had no concept of time, but I knew it had to have been at least a couple of hours since he took me. When he finally opened the door, I recoiled at the sudden burst of light that poured through.

"Don't move and keep your eyes closed." His words echoed around the room.

I did as he told me, I couldn't move if I wanted to, but I kept my eyes shut. I heard him moving around the room, dragging something behind him, rolling it maybe. I felt him getting closer and fought the urge to open my eyes against the sleep threatening to take over again and his instructions. His hair brushed against my cheek and the warmth of his breath cascaded over my shoulder. He picked up a lock of my hair and inhaled deeply.

"Mmm. Jasmine...I like that."

My stomach turned from him being so close. I wanted to cry out, kick him, spit in his face, but I had nowhere to go. Being stuck in this position made me vulnerable, he knew he had me at his disposal. For a brief moment, I thought he walked away. I couldn't hear him or feel him near me. I consider opening my eyes to take a glance at my surroundings, hoping to see a way out. I screech as his icy hands wrap themselves around my ribs. I pull my feet back on impulse and try to use the wall as leverage to move away from him. I want to struggle, turn away from him, wrench myself out of his grasp, but I can't. I no longer have control over my own body. He's too strong. He pushes me against the wall and uses his own body to pin me in place.

I felt the tension in my shoulders ease and as he backed away, my body slid down so my feet touched the floor. My knees buckled and my body crumbled under its own weight. I can hear a sound like metal on metal and I realize he has cuffed me in place. I'm thankful I'm at least able to sit.

I flinched when he touched my face. He rubbed at it in smooth, circular motions. *Was he doing my makeup?* I always preferred a more natural look with a bit of concealer and some mascara. By the time he finished, I felt like my skin was sagging under the weight. Foundation, blush, eyeshadow, lipstick. I tried to imagine what I looked like, if it looked good or if he turned me into a clown. I wanted to laugh at the thought. I knew it was ridiculous, but I'm tired and scared. After only the last few hours, I feel like I'm losing touch with reality.

Rex decided to take the long way to the Carlson's house and pulled up in front of the firehouse. The door was open, but he couldn't immediately see anyone inside. "Hey, Frank." He shouted louder than he meant to and heard the unmistakable sound of metal on metal.

Frank poked his head over the railing of the top lobby area. "Oh, hi Rex. I'll be down in a second." He grabbed a towel off a bench and wiped his face as he walked down the stairs. "What can I do for you?"

"Sorry to interrupt your workout. I just have a few quick questions for you."

Frank narrowed his eyes and his jaw jutted forward. Questions for me? You seem like you're here on official business."

"Yeah. Can you tell me where you were last night?" Rex was uncomfortable having to question him. He had known Frank since he was a baby.

"When I left here, I went home to grab some dinner and then I met Cyrus at the bar around ten. Why?"

"Can you tell me what time you left the bar?"

"Uhh, I don't know. About midnight, I guess. I had to be here first thing. I didn't want to be out too late."

"Did you stop to talk to anyone on your way home? See anyone you know between the bar and your house?"

Frank squinted and Rex could see his tolerance for entertaining him was dwindling. "Rex? Can you just be direct with me? What are you really asking?" He crossed his arms and leaned against the back of the sofa in the lounge area. His T-shirt was damp with sweat.

"Did you see Beth-Ann last night?"

Confusion passed over his face. "No. I saw her earlier this week. Listen, if this is about what I said to Colton yesterday, I didn't mean anything by it. I was just trying to give him a head's up. She's not exactly a child anymore, ya know?"

Rex nodded. "Just so you know, I do have to verify with Ely and Emily that you were there until the time you said you were. I don't want you to think I'm going behind your back." He turned and started to leave.

"Wait a minute. Since when is telling someone his daughter is beautiful an actual crime that you need to investigate?"

Rex paused, let out a slow breath, and turned back. "It's not. Beth-Ann has been missing since last night."

Cyrus shoved a plant onto the nearest shelf to free a hand and pulled his phone from his pocket. "Hey. I can't talk right now."

"You need to. I need to know what's going on with Colton. He just sent Rex in to talk to me."

"Sorry, man. You'll have to ask him yourself. He left here early yesterday and then called this morning and told me he wasn't going to be here today. I had a line wrapped around the store when I opened and it hasn't let up yet." He turned to the side, raising a potted marigold above his head, to move between two customers. "I can't keep up by myself. This is our busiest weekend of the year and he left me to fend for myself. If I survive the day, I may drive to his house and kill him tonight. I've gotta go."

"Just answer one thing..." Cyrus had already ended the call and Frank swore loud enough to send an echo across the firehouse.

Rex always loved visiting the Carlson household. Sally never stopped baking even when she was at home. They always had fresh desserts and the smell of their house made everyone hungry. Rex didn't expect to see Sally since Saturdays were always the busiest day of the week at the bakery. He also expected Walt to be at the post office. He ran half days on Saturdays. No deliveries, but the office was open from eight to twelve and residents could go in to send letters or pick up mail.

He had called Roy earlier to tell him he was going to pay him a visit. Roy agreed to stick around his house until after he spoke to Rex. He pulled right up to the front porch and Roy opened the door before he was able to get out of his truck. The Carlson home was a large, white, country style house with a front porch and bright blue shutters. Flower boxes sat below each window on the first level creating a welcoming aesthetic.

"Hi, Roy. Thanks for sticking around."

"No problem, Sheriff."

"Sheriff? That's different." Having a daughter the same age, most of the children in town referred to Rex as 'Mr. Walker' rather than addressing him as 'sheriff.'

"Official business. I thought it would be appropriate."

Rex nodded his head. "Want to sit out here? It's a nice day."

"Sure. Give me just a minute." He slipped inside and returned with a plate of cookies in hand. "Mom said to make sure you ate some of these." He slid the plate onto a small, wicker table that sat between the two matching chairs.

Rex sat down and selected one from the plate. "White chocolate raspberry? Who am I to argue? He smiled and took a bite. "All right." He motioned for Roy to sit down and removed his notebook from his pocket. "I know this isn't the easiest thing for you, but I need you to be honest and give me as much information as you can. I will ask you for a rundown of the day but first I want you to tell me about the last thing that happened before you and Beth-Ann parted ways for the evening."

"Okay." There was a tremble in his voice that Rex understood to be nerves rather than guilt. "We were arguing. She and Bobby got into a fight, so I was bringing her home. She got really mad at me and made me drop her off at the end of her street. I didn't want to, but she was screaming at me. So, I pulled over and let her out." He dropped his chin to his chest.

"It's okay. I'm not blaming you for anything, I just need you to answer the questions honestly. Any information you give me, even if you don't think it's important, can potentially help me to find her."

Roy nodded but didn't say anything.

"So. You dropped her off at the end of the street. Did you pull onto the street, or did you drop her off at the corner? It's not a far walk to her house, the driveway is right there."

He shook his head and let out a long, slow breath. "No, neither. We were talking so I took the long way around. I didn't drop her off near her driveway. I dropped her off on the other end of the street." He pounded his fist on the table wicker table and the cookies jumped on the plate. "Shit! Why didn't I tell her no? I could have prevented all of this if I had just put my foot down and drove her the rest of the way home." He stood and walked to the porch railing, staring out at the driveway. "This is all my fault."

"No, Roy, it's not. You didn't have any idea what would happen. No one did. But knowing that makes a lot more sense to me now. It's much easier to believe something happened knowing she wasn't in her driveway." He jotted a few notes in his notebook. "I still want a rundown of the evening, but do you think you can show me exactly where she got out?"

He turned to look at Rex, determination on his face. "Yup. I can show you exactly where I dropped her off. It was right in front of the old elm tree with the face carved out in the back."

Rex raised his eyebrow and one side of his mouth curled up. "We have a tree with a face carved in it? How long has that been there?"

Roy shrugged. "I don't know. It's been there as long as I can remember. I can't believe you didn't know it was there. It's funny, but also a little creepy. Wait until you see it."

He sounded more excited than anything and Rex felt he had momentarily forgotten why they were having the conversation to begin with. "We'll head over as soon as I get the rest of the information from you, okay? Come sit back down. We'll try to make this part as painless as possible for you."

They spent the next thirty minutes going over every move from the day before. Roy's recollection of the events matched up perfectly with both Kelsey and Bobby, but Rex learned a little more from when the two of them weren't around. He didn't think any of it was relevant to her going missing, but it was new information and it may mean something in the future.

"Let's take my truck. We'll start at the bonfire location and we'll follow the exact route you took on your way to bring her home. And, if you don't mind, you can show me this face tree."

Roy followed him to his truck and jumped in the passenger's seat. Even though it wasn't the back seat of a police cruiser, it still felt weird to him to be riding in a police vehicle. It somehow made him feel criminal. He reached back and buckled his seatbelt, something he never did while they were riding around town, and sat with his back straight against the seat. His body was stiff and he knew Rex could tell he was uncomfortable.

"Hey. You can relax. I'm not arresting you, I just need your help."

Roy let out a gasp of air. He wanted to relax but his body wasn't allowing it. "Sorry. It's just the idea of being in a police vehicle."

Doesn't bother me." Rex grinned at him.

Roy side-eyed him. "Was that supposed to be some sort of dad joke?" It did make him calm down though. He rolled the window half-way down and sucked in the fresh air while they made their way to the fire pit.

Rex pulled into the lot and stopped his truck. "Would you like to get out for a minute and walk around or do you just want to go?"

What they called the 'lot' was a small clearing that had been destroyed by years of vehicles and foot traffic. It was an empty square of dirt with only an odd weed or two attempting to grow at any given time, sprouting up in a tire track or near the side of a rock. Roy always found it to be a cold, lonely place anytime he drove over without the intention of meeting friends. He pursed his lips and dropped his shoulders. "I'm okay. Let's just go."

"All right. Which way did you go when you left here? I need you to give me exact directions as we drive around."

"You got it. Turn right out of the parking lot."

It took them nearly thirty-five minutes to get around to the end of the road where Roy said he dropped Beth-Ann off. Even taking the long way and driving slowly, this was an extreme amount of time to get anywhere in town. It only took fifteen minutes to drive from one side of town to the other if one were to drive straight through. Beth-Ann only lived two streets down from the fire pit. The town's layout hadn't ever changed. Firmly packed dirt made up the roads and there wasn't a single traffic light. Most of the businesses stood close together on a stretch of the main road with no parking lots or driveways. The houses were the opposite. Each one sat back from the road and had an acre, at least, separating one home from its neighbor. Fields stretched in all directions as far as one could see except for a few wooded areas dotted throughout.

Roy pointed. "There. Stop."

Rex pulled the truck to the side of the road, turned it off, and stood near the front of the vehicle, waiting for Roy to lead the way to the tree. He didn't believe it had anything to do with the case, but he was intrigued and wanted to see what it looked like. He assumed that it would be near the side of the road, but he was wrong. Roy walked into the wooded area and kept going. When Rex turned around, he could barely make out where he parked his truck. He didn't expect to be going on a full hike, but he kept silent and continued to follow Roy. The day was warming up and even in the cover of the trees, tiny beads of sweat started forming on Rex's forehead.

He never spent much of his youth wandering in the woods, aside from the small patch of trees directly behind his house. As a child, he spent most of his time riding his bike through the streets, the fields, and up to the old, abandoned silo he and his friends used as a clubhouse. As a teenager, his group of friends spent most of their time off-roading in their trucks, driving through the fields, causing what the adults called 'innocent trouble.' They weren't supposed to drive through the fields, but no one was ever hurt and they were always easy to spot because they left a cloud of dust in their wake.

After a four-minute walk, Roy stopped. "There it is. On the back of that big tree right there." He pointed to a large one that stood by itself with empty space all around it.

Rex pushed ahead of him and walked around the back side of the tree. "What the hell?" He squinted and moved closer. He could clearly see a face but couldn't make out the rest of the carving. The face was the obvious focal point, the rest more difficult to decipher. There was an 'X' carved in the top and below the face, it looked as if someone tried to carve out a body. It was jagged and jumbled, almost disjointed, like parts of the body had disconnected from others. He took out his phone and snapped a few pictures of what he was seeing. He had never seen anything like it.

"What do you think?" Roy was wide-eyed and jittery like an excited child.

"I'm not sure what to think to be honest. You're right, though. It is fascinating and a bit creepy." They walked back to the truck without speaking. Rex pulled a little red flag from the back of his truck and stuck it in the ground where they entered the woods. "Just in case I need to come back for any reason."

Rex dropped Roy off in his driveway and immediately returned to the spot he had marked with the flag. Without having any leads, the best thing for him to do was a door-to-door canvas to see if anyone saw or heard anything that might be helpful. He reached into his glove box and pulled out a map of the town. A good thing about living in such a small town was the maps were easy to read and update as necessary. On the map, they had every house documented and the laminated cover made it easy to note which houses he spoke to someone and which he needed to revisit. He marked Beth-Ann's house with a big red star and placed a blue arrow on the spot where Roy claimed to have dropped her off. He used the arrow as his starting point with the plan being to visit every house between there and Beth-Ann's home.

It was early afternoon and he hoped to get some good, helpful information from some who may not have realized Beth-Ann was missing. He had plenty of time to stop at all the houses on her street before a late lunch, which he would probably eat in his truck on the way to the next destination. Although he had Beth-Ann's mother, Kimberley, calling around to all their friends and family, he needed to be able to gather information for himself. When he worked in the city, they had trained him to listen for inaccuracies and changes in people's voices. He knew physical signs to look for when someone was lying. If Kimberley were doing what he asked, most residents would expect a visit from him soon. Before turning into the first driveway, he pulled off the road and wrestled his cell out of his front pocket. He called the Peters' house phone and got a busy signal which he took as a good sign. He ended the call and tried Kimberley's cell which she answered on the fourth ring.

"Sheriff? Do you have any information?" She sounded rushed, which Rex translated into her being a tangled mess of nerves.

"I just dropped Roy off and I'm about to start a door-to-door. Any luck on your end?" He didn't expect her to have any useful information. He asked her to make calls as a means to keep her busy. It would give her something to do besides worry while also keeping her from calling him every two minutes asking for updates. It was a trick he picked up years ago which he found to be extremely helpful.

"Nothing yet. Only a couple people admitted, or actually knew, their kids were at the fire last night, but none had any information beyond that."

"Okay. Keep working down the list. And make sure you go back and hit all the numbers where people didn't answer the first time around."

"All right."

"Kimberley? I learned one thing about last night. Roy said he dropped her off, but he told me he didn't drop her off at your house. He dropped her off at the other end of the road."

Her voice went up about three volume levels. "What? Why on Earth would he..."

"Hold on. He feels terrible about it, but they were fighting. You know that, right? He said she told him to drop her off there. Do you have any idea why she would do that?" He heard her sigh heavily through the phone.

"She's stubborn. It's a trait she, unfortunately, inherited from me. If she said the argument was over, it was over. I would have done the exact same thing."

"I'm going to let you get back to making calls, but before I do...do you know anything about the face tree?"

"The what?"

"Fair enough. Let me know if you get any information." He ended the call before she could say anything else. He was glad he wasn't the only one who didn't know about the tree. On its own, it wasn't a big deal, people carved stuff in trees all the time. But there was something about that carving, the way the artist laid out, that was gnawing at his insides. He knew he would go back to see it again before daylight ran out.

Rex stopped at twenty-three houses over the next two hours. He would have to revisit six. So far, he didn't have any more information than he did when he started. He suspected that most people were in bed at that hour and they proved him to be correct. Those who weren't didn't hear or see anything out of the ordinary. It was typical in any investigation, even simple, straightforward ones. People were always quick to answer questions and finish with the police. He adapted quickly to their behaviors in the city. Being in a small town, the benefit was that residents weren't as quick to slam the door in your face. In the past, it would be a day or two before someone would walk into the station, their head hung, and reluctantly tell you they remembered something or they'd admit to knowing something. It happened in every case. Rex hoped Beth-Ann would return before that time came but if she didn't, he would be glad for any additional information people were willing to give.

He drove back to the station to try to piece together what little information he had. He knew it would be a futile effort, but he needed to try. So far, he learned that Roy and Beth-Ann were fighting, he dropped her off at the far end of the street, and there was a tree with a face on it. Aside from being in the general vicinity of where Roy left Beth-Ann, he couldn't imagine what the tree had to do with anything, but he couldn't seem to get it off his mind. One thing being on the police force in the city taught him was if something didn't seem right or gave you that feeling of despair in the pit of your stomach, you needed to follow that instinct. He sat at his desk with his head in one hand and a ham sandwich in the other. He needed to reset his frame of mind back to when he was working in the city. He'd become so accustomed to drunken brawls and false burglar alarms that he almost forgot how difficult it could be when someone's life could be depending on him.

Rex had seen his fair share of death and kidnappings, but it was different in the city. There were cameras everywhere. Even if they couldn't provide a great deal of detail, the grainy images could at least give you a starting point. The city was also busy. As unreliable as witnesses could be, their information could lead you to minor details, help establish a timeline, give you a partial license plate number to run. It wasn't ever much, but it was a place to start. Here, no one had cameras, they didn't have black and white, pixelated images he could try to piece together. There were no witnesses here because wherever you looked, you saw wide open spaces and very few people. In the city, people milled about everywhere, yet most didn't have a group they stayed faithful to. They didn't know their shop owners or even their neighbors. Here, the residents were fiercely loyal to each other and would stay cautious about suspecting any of their neighbors of wrongdoing. Whether close or extended, they acted like family. They trusted each other. Despite a few arguments here and there or a disagreement now and again, the community always rallied together and supported their fellow residents.

"Oscar? Josh?" Get down here, it's time for dinner." The boys stayed locked away in their rooms most of the day. Colton had to keep reminding Kimberley they needed time to process what was happening with their sister. Kimberley's motherly instinct made her want nothing more than to hold onto her children and not let them out of her sight. She only agreed to let them retreat to their rooms when Colton promised her they would have a conversation with the boys during dinner if Beth-Ann hadn't returned yet.

She set the last plate on the table and called up the stairs again. "Boys. We're having pancakes for dinner." She heard both doors open and her two teenage boys scrambled down the stairs. A small smile crept across her face as she grabbed a gallon of orange juice and the syrup from the refrigerator. It was the first time she had smiled all day. Beth-Ann never enjoyed breakfast for dinner and Kimberley didn't like it much, but it was a favorite for Colton and the boys.

Once they were all settled with food on their plates, Colton nodded at Kimberley to start the conversation. "So, guys. Obviously, your sister still isn't home." Her voice caught in her throat and she covered her mouth, fighting back the tears forming in her eyes. She felt Colton's hand cover her own that she had resting on the table. How are you two feeling about the situation?" She let her question hang in the air, wondering if she would get a response from either of them.

Oscar, who was only fourteen, didn't understand the severity of the situation. "If she ran away, can I have her room?" Josh kicked him, hard, under the table. "Ow."

"It's not funny, dipshit. Someone could really have hurt her."

"I was just kidding, geez." His cheeks flushed with pink, either from embarrassment or pain.

"Okay, enough." Colton couldn't handle seeing his kids argue at the moment. "Oscar, do you understand how important and dangerous this situation is?"

The corners of his mouth dropped and his eyes fell to the table. "Yeah. I'm sad that we don't know where she is, and I don't like seeing mom sad. But, it's kind of like she's staying the night at a friend's house. She's hasn't been gone that long." He shrugged and dropped his fork to his plate.

Kimberley's eyes started tearing up again and she fluttered her eyelids trying to blink the tears away. "It's okay to feel that way. Do you understand why your dad and I are so upset?"

He nodded. "Because if she was at a friend's house, you would know where she is and you wouldn't be worried about her."

"That's right. And we need to ask the two of you for help. Did either of you hear her talking to her friends or did she say anything to you about where she was going? Was she complaining about anyone, maybe, making fun of her or giving her too much attention?"

Oscar shook his head and Josh sat staring into space, deep in thought. Josh was two years older than Beth-Ann and more likely to hear about what was going on in her life. Their groups of friends often hung out together.

Colton stopped mid-bite and set his fork down. "Josh? Anything you may have heard through your friends? It doesn't have to be something that came directly from her."

"I mean, there's a lot of guys at school who like her, dad. She's pretty and she's even kind of funny sometimes."

Even in the current situation, hearing Josh say nice things about his sister tugged at Colton's heart. "What about people who aren't at your school?"

Josh took a huge bite of pancake and licked the syrup off his lips. "I did hear her say earlier this week that she thought an older guy was flirting with her, but she was laughing about it. She didn't seem interested at all."

"Do you know who she was talking about? Or talking to?" He could feel the heat rising to his face and he clenched his jaw tight.

"No. She just said someone told her she better be careful when she went off to college because she would have a hard time keeping boys away from her."

Kimberley was soaking up all the information, not surprised that any man would find her daughter attractive.

Colton stood, scraping his chair across the wood floor and excused himself before leaving the room. They all stared at each other, wide-eyed, when they heard the front door slam followed by the door of his truck.

Chapter VI

You're following the script to perfection.

Every time my sister perfected a new dance, my mother and I sat and watched while she put on a show. She never knew that I watched her from the beginning. I knew how hard she worked, the hours she put in. I admired her dedication, loathed the attention it gained.

My mother and sister left me by myself one afternoon, I wanted to see if I could do what she did. I watched her practice for so many hours, I thought for sure I had picked up some of the movements. A few months before, I started holding my hands like hers, mimicking her gestures. That afternoon, for the first time, I picked up one of her puppets. To watch her move them with such ease, how effortlessly she held them up, I never imagined them to be so heavy. The one I chose wasn't her favorite, but mine; adorned in a silver dress with black buttons, lace, and an overcoat. I began with a simple movement, tilting my hand first to the left, then to the right, forward and back. The marionette moved but it was slight, not at all graceful. I tilted the cross brace forward again expecting the puppet to bow. Instead, it took a nosedive straight into the area rug. I straightened the brace and twisted my wrist to the left, hoping for a bend at the waist; the figure crumpled into a broken heap. Thinking the movements might have been too simple, I tried a more complex combination. It was a terrible idea. The puppet spun in the air, the limbs kicked out, its head fell back, and the strings... the strings became a twisted mess. I tried for over an hour to straighten them but succeeded only in making them worse.

She kept most of the puppets, including this one, hung on large hooks screwed into the underside of a long, wooden shelf. I didn't know what else to do, so I hung the puppet in its original place. I retrieved a pair of pliers from the tool drawer in the kitchen and pinched them around the hook. I pulled as hard as I could. The hook put up little resistance and I dropped it directly below. The puppet curled in a ball; strings coiled around its limbs. Satisfied that it looked as if it had fallen on its own, I returned the pliers to the drawer and settled in my room for the rest of the afternoon.

My sagging mattress felt damp against my back from the humidity that never left our house. It was stifling in the summer and the winters brought a bone-chilling cold. Immersed in the book I was reading and fighting the exhaustion that had seeped in, I cringed when I heard a key in the door. I convinced myself my mother would know immediately that I was the one responsible for ruining the puppet. The anxiety coursing through my body made my muscles feel weak, my heart pounded in my chest. The house remained silent longer than I anticipated. With every minute that passed my body relaxed a little more and my concentration on the words in my book became more focused. The first alien had just exited the spacecraft when my sister's ear-piercing scream filled the house. My body jerked, sending my science fiction novel crashing to the ground. I scurried to the corner of my bed, leaning my back against the corner of the walls with my knees pulled into my chest. The commotion coming from her room was more intense than a broken doll warranted and lasted long past the time I stopped counting.

I waited until the screams subsided and the sun had set for the day before I gained enough confidence to emerge from my room. The rumbling coming from my stomach urged me to take the chance. I thought it would be safe since my mother never came storming in as I expected. My sister huddled over the table where the puppet lay splayed, watching our mother perform the magic of untwisting the strings. She looked at me when I entered the room, eyes still damp with tears.

"She fell," she whispered. This was the worst tragedy she had suffered in her short life.

From the disaster in the middle of the table, I knew dinner wouldn't be an option. Standing on my toes, I peered into the cabinet, checking for any signs of mice, before reaching in to grab a packet of crackers. I almost had the door to my bedroom latched when I heard my mother call out to me. My heart rate increased and the sound of rushing blood filled my ears, my skin felt clammy. I pulled the door back just enough so I could see through the crack. My mother approached rapidly and I backpedaled to the middle of my room.

My door flew open hard enough for the doorknob to penetrate the drywall. I backed farther into the room until my dresser abruptly stopped me, the handle from one of the drawers peeled away layers of skin on my back. I heard my mother yelling, saw her mouth moving, but could scarcely make out the words. The back of her hand appeared so fast I didn't have time to react. My shoulder slammed into the dresser, my cheek stung, and my eyes watered. My mother stopped on her way out to the door, turning back to look at me.

"Don't ever touch your sister's things again."

I don't know how she knew it was me. I did everything I could to make it look like an accident and clean up after myself. I don't feel bad about messing up my sister's doll. My mother and sister spent so much time with those stupid toys and I got nothing. An inanimate object got more attention than I did. I vowed then and there I would get my revenge. I didn't know when, but I would get it.

Rex marked the last house off on his map and took a break from canvassing. He swung his truck around to go have another look at the face tree before it got dark. He had to get a better look at the carving. He knew there had to be more to it than what he saw at the first glance. Hours after he first saw it, he still wasn't sure it would help him find Beth-Ann, but he felt drawn to it and needed to get a better look.

It took him longer to find it on his own and he was grateful for the marker he left on the side of the road. The carving faced a small clearing and he approached the tree from a number of different angles, trying to decipher what other elements took their space around the face. Every few feet he took a photo with his phone so he would have something to look back at later. When he finished with the pictures, he knelt in front of the tree, twisted his head in awkward angles, trying to see something he knew was there but couldn't quite make out. It was more than a face, he knew that much, but he couldn't tell if it was something below, above, or beside it. He spent nearly an hour staring at it before he stood on weakened, slightly numb legs. The sun had moved lower in the sky and a cool breeze sent a chill through his body. His stomach grumbled and he took that as a sign to go home, get some nutrients in his body, and talk to his daughter.

Marilyn greeted him when he walked through the door and kissed his cheek while resting her hand on the small of his back. It was a gesture she made any time she was concerned about him. "How are you doing?" She looked at his face, worry embedded in her eyes. She knew how hard Beth-Ann's disappearance would be for him. When they moved back to town, the main reason was because he couldn't handle cases like this one, he struggled with how most of them ended.

"It's been a long day. And it's not over yet." He pulled her into his arms and she could feel the weight of responsibility in his touch. "Lizbeth is home, yes?"

Marilyn nodded as she pulled away from Rex. "She's been in her room all day. She's pretty upset." She removed a pan from the oven and set it on the countertop. "I wasn't sure when you would be home, so I just made some ham and potatoes. I figured you could eat it whenever you wanted."

"Food would be great, I'm starving. I'll go get Lizbeth." Rex knocked on her door and Lizbeth opened it, her eyes red-rimmed and full of tears.

"Did you find her?" Seeing the shake of her head she fell into him, wrapping her arms around his waist and burying her face in his chest.

Rex smoothed the hair on the back of her head. He hated how upset she was but loved the emotional pull in her arms that told him no matter how old she got, she still needed him. "I'm going back out as soon as we eat, but I wanted to talk to you while I'm here."

She lifted her head and looked up at him. "Me? I don't know where she is, dad."

He guided her toward the kitchen. "We'll all talk together."

Once they were settled at the table, Marilyn flashed Lizbeth a sympathetic smile and patted the top of her hand. "How are you doing, sweetie?"

Lizbeth sniffed and shrugged her shoulders. "I'll feel better once I know she's safe. It's not like Beth-Ann to just take off and not say anything." She busied herself by stabbing her potatoes with her fork.

Rex took a deep breath and stared at her. He never minded interviewing or interrogating someone, but he'd never had to do it in his own home before. He felt like he was violating his daughter's privacy. "Lizbeth, I need to ask you a few questions and I need you to be honest with me. Nothing you say will get anyone, including you, in trouble and I promise, whatever you say will be just between us."

Lizbeth looked across the table and squinted her eyes. "Why would I get someone in trouble?"

"Well, because I need to ask you some questions about your friends. Under normal circumstances, you might not be completely honest, or you might omit some details if you think it might get someone in trouble, like if they were doing something they shouldn't be doing. But right now, I need you to tell me everything you know because even the littlest thing might help us find Beth-Ann faster. Can you do that?"

A look of annoyance washed over her face, followed by confusion as she nodded her head.

"Good. Can you tell me when you saw Beth-Ann yesterday? During school, after school, at the party?"

"I saw her at school. We had lunch together and then we had Calculus and Chemistry in the afternoon. We're in the same classes for those."

"And after school?"

"Chemistry is our last class. We walked out together and I waited with her until Kelsey came out and then I left."

"Where did you go?"

"I walked to the pool and then came home after swimming a few laps. Mom was home when I got here."

"Do you know where they went?"

She shook her head. "No. Kelsey said she had homework to do and she always like to get it done early so she can enjoy her weekend."

Mairlyn raised her eyebrows and innocently replied, "Maybe you should hang out with Kelsey more often."

Lizbeth rolled her eyes and looked back at her father. "I don't know where they went, I didn't see either of them again until we all got to the party."

"And what time did you all show up?"

"I don't know. Kelsey had just gotten there when I showed up and Beth-Ann got there a little later. Before you ask, I don't know why she got there late."

Rex had to take a moment to remind himself his daughter's favorite teenage line was 'I don't know.' At least now she was following it up with a little more information. "Okay. Now, I assume you were all drinking while you were there." He watched as Lizbeth's eyes fell to the table. "I don't care about that. I need you to be honest here, was anyone doing anything else besides just drinking?" He stared at her until her eyes met his.

"Yeah." Her voice was little more than a whisper. "I mean some people were smoking, but..."

"You?" He knew he shouldn't have asked that, but his parental instincts kicked in.

"No, dad. Not me."

"Do you know where they got it from?"

She shook her head again. "No. I don't smoke so I'm not usually privy to that information.

It doesn't bother me that people do it, but I don't take part in those conversations. Plus, you know, my dad is the town's sheriff, so people don't really want to talk about that stuff while I'm around."

"Oh, that teenage logic. 'It's fine that she's here partaking in underage drinking, but don't tell her where we get our weed.'" He heard Lizbeth sigh and stopped. "Sorry. Okay. I heard from a number of people that Beth-Ann and Roy were fighting because he didn't tell Bobby they were dating. Is that true?"

"Um. I know they were fighting, everyone at the party could hear them arguing. But I don't know what it was about. I've stayed far away from that weird love triangle, square, circle, they have going on."

Rex had to suppress a smile. "When I spoke to Roy, he told me he dropped Beth-Ann off near the face tree. Do you have any idea why he would have left her there or any information about the tree?"

"They were fighting when they left the party. I don't know why he would have left her there since the tree is far from her house, but if I had to guess? Beth-Ann is very stubborn and she can be a little hot-headed sometimes. If she asked him to stop and he didn't, she would have just opened the door and jumped out."

Rex nodded as she spoke. "And the tree?"

She shrugged. "You probably have as much information about that as I do. I know it exists; it's kind of cool looking. It's been there as long as I can remember."

Rex was thankful he didn't have any other questions for her because as soon as she finished her last sentence, his phone started ringing. "Walker." He pushed his chair away from the table. "I'll head over." He stood, kissed Marilyn on the top of her head and followed suit with Lizbeth. "Thank you for answering honestly. Love you guys. I have to go." He grabbed his keys off the counter and walked out the door.

Rex pulled up outside the firehouse for the second time that day. He heard yelling before he even got out of his truck. He growled to himself, already knowing what the problem was, and walked in, shouting over the other men. All three stopped and looked at him. "What's going on, guys?"

Cyrus stood up from his position on the floor. "When I called, they were just arguing. Then Colton took it too far."

"Both of you. Get up. You really think I have nothing better to do with my time right now?" It wasn't often Rex raised his voice for any reason. When situations forced him to, it commanded respect. Once they were both standing, Rex addressed Colton. "What are you doing here? Why aren't you home with your family?"

Both men wore a sheen of sweat and were breathing heavily. A pink welt was beginning to show next to Colton's eye. "Because my daughter is missing and he knows where she is."

"I told you, I don't."

"Enough!" Rex had never seen Colton angry before in all the years he'd known him. "I talked to Frank this morning, at your request He has an alibi for last night. As a matter of fact, he was with Cyrus at the bar until almost midnight. Ely confirmed that this morning."

"Beth-Ann wasn't supposed to be home until midnight. He could have grabbed her when she was on her way home after leaving the bar."

Frank's face was bright red and his cheekbone was beginning to swell, taking on a purple hue. "I didn't touch your daughter. All I did was make one comment. Yes, I meant it as a warning, but I didn't mean about me. Trust me when I tell you I like women my age and older. And I don't know if you've figured this out or not, but I don't have any trouble getting them to notice me. I don't need to go after a teenager. If I was the type that didn't care about status, I'm pretty sure I could have my pick of any woman in this town, including your wife."

In one motion, Colton turned and connected his fist with Frank's jaw, sending his staggering backwards. Rex and Cyrus both jumped forward between the two men.

Frank found his footing and stood with his shoulders back and hands clenched into fists, his breathing just short of a growl.

Rex pushed Colton away by his shoulders. "What are you doing? Are you trying to force me to arrest you? You know he can press charges for that, right?"

"Did you hear what he said about my wife?"

"Yeah. He's an asshole. We all know that. But that doesn't give you the right to assault him. Now, do you want to continue this charade or are you going to let me get back to looking for your daughter?"

Colton shook his shoulders free of Rex's grip and stomped toward the door.

Rex yelled after him. "You better go straight home."

He turned his head without slowing his pace. "Go find my daughter."

Rex watched him walk out the door before turning back to Frank. "Was that comment about his wife really necessary?"

"Hey. I'm an asshole. You all know that."

He raised his eyebrows and nodded once in a way that said, 'touché.'

"Listen, Rex. I don't know where she is. Yes, okay, she's kind of hot. But, she's also a kid. I'm not into that. I barely liked teenagers when I was one."

"Fine. Are you pressing charges against Colton or forgetting about it.?"

"I get that what I said about his daughter probably wasn't in the best interest of anyone, but the only thing I'm pressing is an ice pack to my face. He's upset; his daughter is missing. I can't say I would have acted any differently."

Rex left the firehouse not feeling any better about the situation between the two men and no closer to finding Beth-Ann. The sun had set since he's arrived and the darkness brought along a cool air that sent a chill through his body.

Chapter VII

You will dance for me. I am in control.

The next time he came in, I wasn't glad to see him, but I would give almost anything for the clothing I saw in his hands. The room was stark and I could feel the cold seeping into my bones. I was so cold I ached. He unlocked the clasp that had me attached to the wall and raised my arms above my head. I don't know how, but I started moving up, to about the same height I was before. My eyes were still adjusting to the light, but I caught a glimpse of plum and a light lilac color as the heavy, silken fabric brushed over my skin.

He slipped the dress on, under my feet, and pulled all the way up. I didn't know if the whole thing was homemade, but I knew the fasteners were. He pushed the front against me and reached around to pull up the zipper that started at the top of my buttocks and went all the way to my neck. He wrapped the sleeves around my arms and stuck them together with Velcro. He moved away and I could feel his eyes burning into me. He approached again, reached his hand into the top of the dress and, in turn, reached below each breast and gently lifted each to make my cleavage more prominent above the neckline.

Satisfied with his work, he began wrapping a skein of rope around each of my limbs in what felt like a wild, knotted mess. He reached behind me again and attached the ropes to what I could only assume was a pulley of sorts. I felt the ropes tighten, thankful he hadn't put any around my neck or my stomach, as I rose from my current position to about four feet higher. He left me there, alone, terrified, for the next several hours.

The old church stood at the end of the main street. It was the last building before the town line. Pastor Timothy Williams stood outside the doors, greeting residents as they walked in. The number of churchgoers varied week by week. For some, it was part of their weekly routine, others went when they felt they needed to. As long as Timothy had lived in town, he'd never seen so many people on a Sunday morning. News of Beth-Ann's disappearance spread around town fast and almost every resident showed up to pray for her well-being and safe return.

Timothy spent three hours the previous evening rewriting the sermon on the off chance that Beth-Ann didn't show up by morning. The doors remained open during the service to allow everyone to hear, even if they didn't have a seat. The pews and aisles were full and a small crowd gathered outside the entrance. Rex chose to stay outside, behind the crowd, to observe the people and their behaviors.

When the service ended, Rex made his way to the door, waiting for Pastor Timothy to take his spot outside. He shook his hand and leaned forward, whispering in his ear. "I'm going to stand next to you to look for any signs of odd behavior."

The high, spring sun caused the pastor's hair to sparkle like silver in the light. "You do what you need to if it gets Beth-Ann home safely."

Rex watched a lot of handshakes and heard many "thank yous" and "that was a lovely sermon" passed back and forth. Jim was the next person to come outside, his hand on his daughter's shoulder. It was rare that Rex saw him in anything other than a T-shirt, flannel shirt, or baseball cap. Owning and running a farm didn't leave much time for him to socialize or have reason to dress up. He wore a blue button-down shirt with the sleeves rolled up and khaki pants.

"Jim, I'm so glad you could join us today." The pastor shook his hand and turned his attention to Kelsey, who was dabbing her eyes with a tissue. "Kelsey, I can't imagine the pain you're feeling now. But keep the faith. I feel in my heart she'll come home soon."

"Thank you." She barely managed to choke the words out. She stayed strong and tried to remain positive until she saw how many people came to the church. Seeing that many people concerned about Beth-Ann's whereabouts made it too real for her. Jim wrapped his arm around her shoulders and led her to the truck, followed by her brothers and mom.

Ely and Emily were the next out with Sue Ellen and Mary Jane at their side. Timothy knew them all by name but had never seen any of them inside the church. "It's nice to see you all here. I know it'll make Beth-Ann happy to know everyone came out."

Emily smiled at him, but it looked more like a smirk. Her facial expressions always gave away what she was thinking even when the words she spoke didn't match. "We came out for the girls. Mary Jane is the same age as Beth-Ann and Sue Ellen isn't much younger. They all hang around together, so we wanted to show our support. Kimberley is beside herself with worry."

"I understand. She's lucky to have a friend like you." He wiped beads of sweat from his forehead with the back of his hand. "Mary Jane, stay strong and pray for Beth-Ann's return." He smiled wide when he looked at Sue Ellen. "Sue Ellen, you look more like your mom every day."

The tone in his voice caught Rex's attention. His nerves already had him on edge and he felt something underlying in the way Timothy made that statement. He had to remind himself that Timothy was a pastor and probably didn't have any ill intention. He was getting anxious; the service took longer than he expected and he wasn't getting anything helpful from the conversations he overheard. Kimberley and Colton were the last to exit. Rex patted Timothy's arm to let him know he was leaving. It was respectful to let them have a conversation without anyone listening.

Rex spent the afternoon driving around town, interviewing all the teenagers who were at the bonfire Friday night. All their stories matched and the one solid piece of evidence he had was that Roy was the last person to see Beth-Ann.

He went home for the evening, feeling defeated. He wanted to force his way inside every house in town, check every room, basement, and attic until he found her. It had only been one day and the stress was threatening to overwhelm him. He couldn't begin to imagine what Kimberley and Colton were going through, he had a daughter the same age that he was worried about, and he knew the entire town was looking at him to solve Beth-Ann's disappearance.

Marilyn greeted him at the door when he got home. She'd curled her short hair into wide beach waves and put on makeup that gave her a welcoming glow. Behind her, a lit candle stood on the kitchen table along with two wine glasses and a bottle of red wine.

"You look incredible." Rex wrapped his arm around her waist and pulled her close, leaning in for a deep kiss. "What is all this?"

"Well, I thought you could use a bit of stress relief. I know these last two days have been hard on you."

"They have and it doesn't look like my days are going to get any easier. I've been interviewing people for two days and haven't gotten any closer to finding her." He stopped talking and his jaw dropped. "Um. Where is Lizbeth" His breathing sped up and he could feel his heart beating.

Marilyn reached forward and put a hand on his arm. "Don't worry. She's spending the night at Mary Jane's. She wanted to be with her friends and Emily is more than happy to have her. Both her and Ely are home because they close the bar on Sundays. She's going to call before she goes to bed and before she leaves for school. Rex? Look at me. She's fine. I walked her into the house myself and trust me, Emily is not letting those kids out of her sight."

"You're sure Ely is home with them?"

"I'm sure. Now, let's eat dinner before it gets cold. We can have a couple glasses of wine, you can take a nice, hot shower, and then I'll give you a back rub. Maybe we'll even take advantage of having an empty house."

Emily and Ely sat all three girls down on the couch. Their house was the most modern of any others in town. The walls had been painted a medium gray with dark gray trim. They furnished the living room with a black leather couch, matching armchairs, and a metal table with a glass top. The flat screen television took up half the wall opposite the seats.

Ely leaned forward, resting his elbows on his knees. "Girls, we need your help. Lizbeth, obviously, your dad is the sheriff and I know it may not always be the easiest thing to talk to him, especially if you think you may get someone in trouble. But, I don't think we have to tell you all how important this is. I don't care who it is, what it pertains to, I don't even care if something that happened is completely illegal. Let us figure that piece out. Is there anything, at all, that you can think of that might help Sheriff Walker find Beth-Ann?" His t-shirt allowed both sleeves of tattoos to show and the skull pendant he wore around his neck swayed back and forth as he spoke.

Sue Ellen was the first to respond. "I don't know what you're asking. Sheriff Walker asked us earlier and we told him everything we know about Friday."

"Right, but what about before Friday? Was she upset about anything? Was she hanging out with anyone new? Did she talk to anyone that you thought was unusual?" Between the two, Ely was softer spoken and his tone had a caring quality to it. Emily was much more direct and matter of fact. "Was she doing drugs, drinking, seeing someone behind Roy's back?"

"Ugh, mom." Mary Jane rolled her eyes. "None of us are like that. The only people I can think of that she talked to, without anyone else around, are Cyrus and Frank. But, she sees Cyrus all the time at the store and Frank was just being Frank."

"What does 'being Frank' mean, exactly?" Emily spoke first, cutting Ely off.

"It means he was being gross like he always is. You know, telling her how pretty she is and how all the guys are going to love her when she goes away to college. It doesn't really mean anything. He does it to everyone."

"Yeah, well, 'everyone' is a little different when you're talking about teenagers. This is the sort of thing we need to know about. If any of you think of anything else, you need to let us know. That includes you, Lizbeth."

Ely went to the kitchen and grabbed his coat and keys off the rack on the wall.

"Hey." Emily followed him. "Where are you going?"

"Where do you think? He can't talk to our girls like that and get away with it."

"No, I get that, but the girls aren't wrong. He really does hit on every female he sees. He hits on me all the time."

"That doesn't count. Everyone hits on you."

Emily rolled her eyes. "Say something to Rex if you're concerned. But don't start shit with Frank. It's not going to change who he is."

Chapter VIII

Your beliefs won't help you. They hold no power here.

I may have killed my sister.

I chose to play in her room, I like it more than my own. Like with everything else, she always gets the best. Her room is larger than mine, has a bigger bed with a frame while my small mattress lies directly on the floor. She has a new, fluffy comforter and I wrap my threadbare blanket around myself multiple times for warmth. Her dresser and additional shelving units have room to display all her dolls. I use a cardboard box for a hamper and my dresser is so old it's missing the bottom two drawers.

I took a toy truck I found in a parking lot weeks ago and ran it along the dingy living room carpet and into her room. My mother gave me trouble for plucking the truck from the middle of a mud puddle. She couldn't understand why I would want to play with such a thing; why I couldn't have better taste, like my sister. She wanted to know why I couldn't find something better to occupy my time. I didn't have any friends. Girls were starting to gain the interest of other boys my age. If they were anything like my mother and sister, I didn't understand the appeal. Beside her bed, my sister had a blue and purple braided rug in the shape of an oval; the perfect makeshift track to drive the truck around. As I maneuvered around one turn for what I was sure was the fiftieth time, I lost my balance due to my crouched position. My shoulder slammed into the dresser, and I heard wood splintering and the crack of porcelain as the face of one of the dolls met the floor. I froze in fear, knowing my mother would be home soon. I heard my sister's scream rush in from the kitchen. I wasn't supposed to be here. I'm not allowed in her room. I stayed in the position I had fallen into, hoping she would remain in the kitchen.

The bedroom door flew open and bounced off the wall behind it. Her eyes fell on the doll that landed in a heap on the floor. She screamed again and rushed forward. I stood, trying to stop her before the downstairs neighbors heard her screaming. The top of her foot caught the side of mine and her speed propelled her forward. She couldn't stop the momentum. Her head hit the window first, sending shards of glass to the ground outside and her body followed, landing with a heavy thud. My breath caught in my throat. I took a tentative step forward and stopped. The door to our house slammed shut and I heard the clash of my mother's keys hit the shelf in the entryway. My chest and throat constricted as I struggled with my body's desire to vomit. I made my way to the window, quickly, quietly, and stuck my head out, careful to avoid the remaining glass spikes protruding from the frame. My sister's body lie crumpled on the muddied ground below. She looked like one of her dolls when she lowered them a little too much and their limbs wobbled and collapsed, bent in unnatural positions.

My muscles weakened, I didn't know whether to call my mother and tell her what happened or sneak to my room and pretend I didn't know. I backed up straight, avoiding the glass again, turned, and slammed into my mother. She didn't say a word. Her hands gripped my upper arms hard and she tossed me into the side of the bed before rushing to the window. I was thankful to have hit the mattress, but my knee smashed against the bed frame, my side scrapped against it as I fell. I sat there, trembling, waiting for the punishment that was sure to come. I hardly noticed my mother rushing out the door.

Ruth was busy filing her weekly paperwork when Kent came down the stairs. She stood and ironed down the front of her khaki skirt with her hands. This was the second year he visited her hotel and he already booked in for three more weekends before the end of the summer. Kent and his son arrived the previous evening and Ruth put a bit more effort into her appearance this morning. She dried her red bob so it fell straight and curled in just at the very ends, put mascara on her lashes, and added a small amount of blush to give her cheeks some color.

The last time she saw him, in early fall, they spent a wonderful evening together having dinner in the city and she hoped to continue where they left off. They kept in touch over the last few months, talking at least once a week. Ruth was glad he was back in town but wasn't overjoyed about him bringing his son with him this time. She didn't like the idea of him having a son at all. Having children meant having another woman in his life somewhere.

"Good morning, young lady." He wore a peach-colored polo and gray cotton pants. His outfit screamed spring.

Ruth felt the heat rise to her face. "Good morning to you. Are you heading out for the day already? It's so early."

"Not yet. I came to see if I could convince you to join me for dinner later."

She remembered what attracted her to him to begin with. He stood with his shoulders squared and his head held high, even the tone of his voice exuded confidence. "I would love to." She didn't want to ask the follow-up question but felt she had no choice. "Will Dustin be joining us?"

He shook his head. "No. I asked if he minded and he told me he'd be fine going to the diner. So, it'll be just the two of us." He winked at her. "Is Italian, okay?"

"Italian would be great." After they agreed on a time, Ruth watched him walk back to his room and spent the next hour grumbling about him asking his son if he minded. *Was he asking a sixteen-year-old child for permission?* They weren't even officially dating and Ruth already felt like she was coming in second.

Dustin left the hotel just before it started to get dark. Kent offered him a ride to the diner and he declined. His dad only just introduced him and Ruth and he took an immediate dislike to her. When introduced, she said 'Hello,' and nothing more before stepping between father and son and locking her elbow with Kent's. Dustin found it rude and was embarrassed for her, being so possessive of a man she hardly knew.

The diner was a farther walk than he thought and he almost turned back before he saw

Clint, Jimmy, Sue Ellen, and Sarah. Without thinking, he approached the group. "Holy shit, there are people my age in this town. I'm Dustin." He reached his hand out toward Clint who reciprocated and shook it.

"I'm Clint. This is Jimmy, Sarah, and Sue Ellen. Did you just move here or something?"

"Nah. My dad travels for work and he asked if I wanted to come with him. He doesn't enjoy the city much, so he always finds places to stay in small towns. It's my first time coming with him and I'm so bored. What do you do for fun out here anyway?"

Clint shrugged. "It's small-town living, we make our own fun. We usually have a party on the weekends, although I don't think we'll be doing that for a while. We run our trucks through the fields as long as there's no snow. But mostly, we just hang out at someone's house."

"That sounds awful."

"You can see for yourself. Hop in. We have a little time before we have to be home." Sarah and Clint climbed into the cab of the truck while Dustin, Sue Ellen, and Jimmy hopped into the bed.

They weren't out long. Clint took them on one lap around an open field before driving back to the pharmacy.

"That was way more fun than I thought it would be." Dustin eyes were wide and he could feel the dust coating his face. "Although, I'm sure I'll have a giant bruise on my shoulder in the morning. I thought for sure you were going to throw me out of the back at one point."

"We told you." Jimmy took an instant liking to Dustin.

Sue Ellen nudged Dustin with her shoulder. She also took a liking to him, a different kind than Jimmy. "Do you want to grab an ice cream with me? We still have time to get one before the pharmacy closes."

He smiled at the invitation and then squinted. "You can get ice cream in the pharmacy?"

"Yeah. It's a small town, remember?"

"I have to get home. My mom will kill me if I'm late. She didn't even want me to come without Bobby."

"That's okay. Clint can bring you home. I'll just walk to the bar when we're done and I'll ask my dad for a ride home."

Jimmy grunted. "I don't think we should leave you. Our mom will probably be mad if we do."

"It's right next door. I can see it from here." After more protests, Sue Ellen got her way and she and Dustin spent the next thirty minutes sitting at the counter, drinking milkshakes, and discussing how different their lives were.

Jake was surprised to see the teens come in so late, but he never minded last minute business. "Hate to do this to you, kids, but it's closing time.

Sue Ellen, do you need a ride home? It'll just take me a few minutes to close up."

"No, thanks. I'm going to walk over and ask my dad. He'll give me a ride."

"If you're sure. I know it's close, but be careful."

"I will." She hopped off the stool and her and Dustin heard the click of the lock closing on the door behind them.

"Why is everyone so against you being by yourself? Is it me?"

She sighed and then laughed. "No, it's not you. One of our friends went missing about a month ago and she hasn't come home yet, so our parents and all the adults are freaking out thinking every teenager is going to get kidnapped. Like, I get it, but..."

"Oh, that's...you're not afraid to be by yourself? It's dark out."

Her eye roll told him everything he needed to know but she replied anyway. "No. My parent's own the bar that's right there." She pointed to the next building down the street. "We have streetlights and it's right there. If I yell right now, they'll be able to hear me."

"Okay." He stared at the ground and kicked at the dirt with the toe of his shoe. "Um. I am heading the other way, but I can walk with you if you want?"

Grateful for the dark corner, she felt her cheeks turn pink. "That's okay. But maybe we can meet up again tomorrow? I can come find you at the hotel after school."

"Sounds good."

They walked in opposite directions. Only one made it to their destination.

Chapter IX

Forever the bridge that connects us all. But strings connect us, too.

"Well. You're not the one I was hoping for, but you'll do."

I can't open my eyes and all my muscles hurt. A scream got stuck in my throat when he ran his hands up my thighs.

"I was looking for your sister. Her appearance fits my aesthetic better, but I can work with you. I think I even have a dress that will fit you perfectly."

I can hear him leave the room and I struggle against the drugs that are in my system. I feel like I'm floating, but not freely. Suspended is more accurate. I'm hanging, face down, with my arms out wide.

"I was right. It's just the right size and this color is perfect for you." He wraps the material around me and I can hear Velcro as he places it and rips it open again to reposition it. The bodice is so tight, I feel like I can't breathe. He steps away and I can feel him staring at me.

With all the energy I could pull together, I find my voice. "Why are you doing this?"

He huffed. Then he laughed. "I'm doing it because I can."

His response sends a shiver through my body. It told me he was willing to do anything he wanted and didn't care about the outcome.

Emily pounded on Rex's front door with the side of her fist. "Sheriff?" She yelled over and over.

He opened the door, rubbing an eye with one hand. One tuft of hair stuck straight up and he had stubble from multiple days of not shaving on his chin. "Emily? Is everything okay? It's two-thirty in the morning."

"Sue Ellen didn't come home. Ely is out looking for her. She was out with a few friends and they left her with some weird guy and now she hasn't come home. If he hurt her, Rex, I swear I'll kill him, whoever it is." Even in what was sure to be one of the scariest moments of her life, Emily stayed true to her character. She wasn't crying or inconsolable, she was angry. She was proof of what Rex tried to get across to profilers when he was working in the city. He believed there were typical emotions that presented in most people during certain situations, but he didn't believe all people reacted the same way.

He opened the door wide and gestured for her to come in. Going to the kitchen, he pulled a chair out for her while he went to fill a kettle with water. He was the sheriff, but he never forgot his manners as a host. "Oh, you prefer coffee, don't you?"

"Please."

"Okay. Start at the beginning. Give me every detail of information you have, starting from when she left your house." He went about filling the coffee pot and pulled a notebook out of the kitchen drawer while it brewed. He sat and jotted quick notes while she continued with the details.

"She went out with Clint, Jimmy, and Sarah. They didn't want to leave her, but she insisted. They said they left her with some kid that's staying at the hotel. Damian, Daniel, Dalton, something like that. It began with a 'D.' They said they all just met him last night and he seemed like an okay kid. Sue Ellen stayed behind with him and got some ice cream at the pharmacy. She told all of them she was going to walk to the bar after to ask Ely for a ride home."

"Did she ask him?"

"She never made it."

"Where is Ely now?" It just hit him that they wouldn't have gotten home that long ago.

"On his way to the hotel to confront that kid. Once we realized Sue Ellen wasn't home, I went to June and Randy's to ask Sarah and Ely brought Mary Jane to Suzanne and Jim's to talk to Jimmy and Clint. He left Mary Jane there with Kelsey."

Rex had to stop himself from shaking his head. It was never a good idea for a father to confront someone he thought may have hurt his daughter. "I don't like that he went off on his own. As a father, I understand, but he should have called me." He poured two cups of coffee, one in a mug which he set in front of Emily and another in a travel mug for himself. "Go ahead and drink your coffee. I'm going to wake Marilyn up and she'll bring you home. I want you to stay there in case she comes back."

Emily took huge gulps of coffee while she waited for Marilyn and Rex. "Where are you going?"

"To find your husband before he does something stupid." Rex grabbed his keys and walked out the door, smoothing his hair down as he went. He had known Ely for years and thought he was a good guy. He also knew him well enough to know if anyone hurt either of his daughters, Ely would act first and think second.

"You can tell me or I'll start knocking down every door in here until I find him."

Rex heard Ely from outside the hotel door. He must have woken Ruth as soon as he got there, which was a sign it would be a worse night than he already anticipated. He took a deep breath before walking through the door, not willing to entertain Ruth and her mightier-than-thou attitude. "Ruth." The name came out loud enough to wake every guest. "It's not a request. Tell us which room he's in."

She rolled her eyes and sighed with a dramatic flair. "I should have known you'd show up. He's in 203." She didn't want Kent involved, but if his son were in trouble, maybe it would force him to have to stay longer. That, she was okay with.

Rex brought Dustin down to the station to question him before Ely had a chance to rip him to shreds. His story matched what Emily had already relayed to Rex. He added what happened after everyone left, including going to get ice cream, asking if Sue Ellen wanted him to walk her to the bar, and then going their separate ways. According to his story, he was the last one to see her. The problem Rex found with that was he wasn't in town when Beth-Ann disappeared and neither was his father.

He put a call out to Jim and Randy and asked them to keep the kids home until he had a chance to question them. He didn't consider it a waste of time because he wouldn't get any helpful information if he didn't interview them, but their stories matched. Once again, he had nothing to go on. The girls just vanished.

He went back to the station and made the phone call he had been dreading. One girl was one thing, but now that a second had gone missing, he had to admit he needed help. He called his old captain and put in a request for a couple competent detectives. The captain assured him they would be in town first thing the next morning.

The town hall held meetings once a month. There were about fifteen regulars who attended every meeting with others going when the topics of discussion were of interest to them. Tonight, they had a full house and most were waiting for updates from Rex. He ran through the door a few minutes before the meeting commenced and he heard bits and pieces from residents grumbling about him not doing enough and not being competent enough. They called the meeting to order and the first comment was from Ruth. She had a lot of opinions for someone who didn't have any children.

"I want to know why we continue to allow Sheriff Walker to keep his job when he clearly isn't doing it correctly. He hasn't even found the first girl yet and now another one is missing. Last night, he came into the hotel and harassed me until I told him which room a guest was staying in because his son had a conversation with that girl. It's ridiculous." There were murmurings of agreement coming from all over the room.

Rex had been clenching and unclenching his fists and practicing his calming breathing techniques while she spoke to stop himself from calling her out on her lies and her behavior. When she stopped her rant, she sat down and Rex went to the microphone in the front of the room. "If I may have the floor...I understand parents, especially those of girls, are scared. I want to assure you I'm doing everything I can to find them. I have called in back up and expect them first thing tomorrow morning. In the meantime, I urge you all to keep a close eye on your children and not let them go out alone, especially at night. And Ruth, for the record, the first girl's name is Beth-Ann and 'that girl' who went missing last night? Her name is Sue Ellen. They're people, living human beings. If you're going to pretend to care, at least put some effort into it. Thank you." Attendees shouted questions at him as he walked to the back of the room and out the door. He felt he said enough. Ruth's tantrum at the beginning put him on edge and made his blood boil.

He drove straight home, determined to get some sleep so he would be coherent enough to fill the new detectives in on everything he knew so far. For the second time that day, he had to admit he needed help. After Ruth's outburst, he wasn't thinking straight. He should have stuck around to observe who was in attendance and who wasn't.

Chapter X

*You were the wrong half of what I wanted but your interest
intrigued me.*

I didn't see my mother for three weeks after my sister's dive out the window. I spent my time locked away in my room, only leaving the confined space to get a snack or go to school. I learned to get myself up and ready in the morning, my mother could never bother to help. I assumed she was home when I left for school and when I arrived home, but I couldn't be sure. She hadn't made a real meal in weeks and we were down to scraps in the cabinet and slices of fuzzy cheese in the refrigerator. I didn't know if my mother was eating, but I didn't care either way. My stomach had gone from the occasional growl to groaning and cramping. I only owned two pair of pants, a pair of secondhand orange corduroys and jeans with patches on the knees and back pocket. I now had to hold both pairs up with a tie I pulled off the living room curtains.

I could tell when my mother started going out again because her keys moved in position on the shelf. I came home one day to find a box of crackers sitting on the table. It wasn't much, but I carried the whole box to my room and somehow managed to make them last for three days before I began dumping crumbs into my mouth from the bottom of the wrappers. The next day, when I got home from school, I saw my mother standing in the doorway.

"You have five minutes. Put what you're taking in this bag and get in the car."

She pushed past me, shoving the bag into my chest, and stomped down the stairs. I heard the car door slam once she got in. *What I'm taking? Where are we going?* I had no idea what I should take or how I was supposed to fit anything in one plastic grocery bag. I went to my room and stuffed as much as I could into it. The sides began to strain and rip. What I couldn't fit in the bag, I packed in my pockets before putting on some extra layers of clothing. *What if we weren't coming back?* I draped what items I could over my arms and shuffled out to the waiting car. Gravel kicked up from the back tires before I had a chance to close my door. I had to guess my mother cleaned out the entire house while I was away at school. She piled the bags in the backseat so high I couldn't see out the back window.

We rode in silence for four hours before I gained the courage to ask where we were going. My mother glanced at me, annoyed that I spoke. "We're moving, far away from where we were so no one can ask questions about your sister."

"Why would they ask questions? She's dead." My eyes watered first, followed by the throbbing in the bridge of my nose. It happened so fast; I never saw her raise her hand.

"Don't you ever, ever say that again. Do you hear me?"

All I could do was squeak my agreement. My voice caught in my throat from trying not to cry. I would never mention my sister again.

We drove for three more hours. I fell asleep once, waking with stiff muscles in my legs and a sore neck. I couldn't wait to get out of the car to stretch. I finally got the chance once we pulled into the driveway of our new house. As I expected, it didn't look any better than the one we left. I hoped it would be nicer when I got to see it in the daylight. I followed my mother's lead and walked to the porch. The smell of mold hit me in the face when she opened the door. It was cold outside, but the smell was so strong I wanted to turn back and sleep in the car. At least I would be able to breathe out here. I crept toward the doorway and poked my head in, gasping when my mother hit the light switch. Yellowed wallpaper curled away from the wall at every seam and corner, a thick spiderweb coated a light fixture hanging in the middle of the room, and the floorboards groaned in defiance from the weight of my slight frame. A cool breeze continuously circled through the room even after I closed the door. There were no open windows, the house was old and in disrepair.

Our old house was small and dark, but I didn't mind the limited space. This one is huge in comparison, it has nine rooms, including one my mother told me is for food storage. I wondered what we would use it for. Upstairs, my mother gave me the choice of two bedrooms, a large one across the hall from her's, or a smaller one at the end of the hall. I chose the smaller one. It had a view that looked into the woods behind the house and I liked that it was the furthest away from her. Directly next to her bedroom was a closed door. My mother pointed to it, told me it was off limits, and forbade me to ever open it. I nodded in understanding and slunk off to my room.

Rex arrived at the station early, ready to welcome the new detectives. He made sure his evidence board was up to date with the latest disappearance. He wasn't happy about it, but the only person he had left to talk to about Sue Ellen was Bobby. Somehow, he was the only person in town that couldn't account for his whereabouts during the timeframe he was looking at. He heard a car pull into the lot and went to the front door to greet the two men.

The driver was tall, well-built, and Rex guessed a few years older than himself. The passenger was the opposite, short, thin, and looked barely out of school. They were grumbling amongst themselves while they walked toward Rex.

"Sheriff Walker? I'm Martin, this is Parker." Rex could tell from the introduction that Martin was the senior detective in their duo.

"Nice to meet you. I really appreciate you two coming to assist."

Martin pushed by Rex on his way inside. "They could have warned us what we were getting ourselves into. This town has a population of about three hundred people, the girls probably ran away just to have more human interaction. I don't know who we pissed off, but the captain is going to hear about this." Martin dug a toothpick out of a pocket and stabbed it between his teeth while he looked at the evidence board. "Okay, I see the two missing girls. Where are your suspects?"

They hadn't been in town more than three minutes and Rex was already regretting his decision. Martin's tone was gruff and demeaning. "That's why I called asking for help. I only have three and I don't believe any of them are actually guilty."

"So, you have three people who aren't suspects?" It was the first time Parker spoke and his voice matched his size.

"I'm bringing one in for questioning today. But two of the three are kids, teenagers. Even if they were capable of committing the crime, I don't believe they have the mental capacity to keep up with all the stories and lies they would have had to tell."

"Okay, run down the list. Who are you looking at?"

The last time he checked, Rex was still the sheriff of Dunmeyer. He had already reminded himself twice that he needed the help and he asked for this. He needed to put his feelings about Martin aside. "The first one is Roy. The only reason he's on the list is because he was the last person to see Beth-Ann before she went missing and he was also dating her. They were arguing the night she disappeared. Next, is Bobby. He's the one I'm going to bring in for a formal interview today. He happens to be Beth-Ann's ex and he has no alibi for the night Sue Ellen disappeared. He claimed he was 'just driving around.' Lastly, Frank. He's our town's firefighter. He's got a temper on him and he's made some inappropriate comments lately about some of the younger girls in town."

"And no one has beat him to a bloody pulp yet? Interesting."

"Oh, he's gotten into a few fights about it. He admits to making the comments and he'll tell you himself that he's an asshole, but I don't believe he's capable of actually doing anything harmful. I've known him his entire life."

"Well, you should know better than that. Regardless of how, or how well you know someone, you never truly know them. I think I'll go pay him a visit first."

They spent the next two hours going over Rex's notes. Martin pulled down the evidence board and reset it so it was more to his liking. He added names of people to talk to and made some notes in his own notebook. Parker was listening and asked a question here and there, but seemed more interested in anything else. He stared at the ceiling, touched the corners of each desk, restacked piles of paperwork, and walked in and out of the station on three different occasions. Rex, once again, regretted his decision to ask for help.

"We're going to go have a little conversation with our new friend Frank. Why don't you go get this Bobby fellow and we'll meet you back here."

Rex wasn't planning to talk to Bobby until after the school day ended. There were only two days left and he didn't want to pull him from class. He rolled his eyes and stood up. "I'll meet you back here."

He didn't get half-way to Bobby's house when his cell phone rang. "Good morning, Pastor."

"Sheriff. Not a social call, I'm afraid. I need you over at the grocers. Ely is causing a ruckus."

Rex slammed on his brakes. "I'll be there in less than five." He let a car pass, made a three-point turn, and headed back toward Bill's store.

When he walked in, he saw Ely with Bill pinned to one of the shelves.

"I will kill you where you stand if you did anything to hurt my daughter." Spittle flew from his mouth and landed on Bill's chin. He only gave about two inches of space between them. Ely's face was bright red and glistening. His fists were clenched and his muscled forearms were defined.

Bill's face, in contrast, was ghostly white. He was much shorter than Ely and was curling in on himself in a shy, protective manner. Bill didn't often make enemies, he mostly kept to himself, and Ely was one of the last people he would want as an enemy. "I swear, I didn't do anything. I only stopped because I saw her walking by herself."

"So, you thought she was an easy target?"

"No, of course not. I stopped to see if she was okay." His voice trembled while he spoke. "I thought the kids weren't supposed to be out by themselves."

"They're not because of creeps like you. What were you even doing over that way? You live in the opposite direction."

"That's none of your business. I'm allowed to do things when I'm not at work."

"I've known you for years, Bill. You never do anything outside of work." His voice was still raised, but the color of his face changed from red to a deep pink.

Neither of the men noticed Rex until he interrupted them. "Ely. Back up. What's the problem?"

Ely turned and stared at him, contemplating whether to continue yelling or speak to him in a calmer tone. "He saw Sue Ellen the night she went missing. He pulled over and talked to her."

"Bill?"

"I already told him. I did see her and I did talk to her. All I did was ask if she was okay. She told me she was fine and she was walking to the bar so Ely could give her a ride home."

"And?"

"That's it. She said she was fine, I left."

Rex let out a long breath. "Ely, go home. Why are you even out this early?"

"Because I got an anonymous message this morning letting me know that he saw her. Why he's going around telling everyone, I have no idea." He turned back to Bill. "Is it because my wife refused your offers for lunch and coffee? Getting your revenge by taking my daughter?"

"That's enough, Ely. Go home. I'll stop by later to talk with you."

He walked toward the door and turned back one more time, pointing at Bill. "If you even so much as look at Mary Jane, I'll kill you and mount your head above the bar as a trophy."

Rex let him leave. He'd talk to him about the threat he made when he went to his house later. "Bill, what were you doing over in that direction the other night?"

"I was...visiting with a lady friend." His cheeks turned pink at the admission.

"A lady friend?" Rex's eyebrows drew together. "There are no single woman over on that side of town."

Bill sighed and his shoulders dropped. "I met her at the hotel. She comes in once a month and I go over to see her."

"What's her business that she comes into town so often?" He needed to ask, though he wasn't sure he wanted to know the answer.

"We have an agreement. She comes to town, I pay for her hotel room, I go visit her to do what we do, and that's it."

"So, she's a prostitute?"

"I prefer to think of her as an escort with benefits. We talk, too." Now that he was being honest, he didn't seem as shy about the situation.

"Okay, but if she's only here once a month, it would make sense to spend as much time with her as you can. Sue Ellen went missing rather early in the evening. Where you going to the hotel or heading home?"

"I was heading home. We had a misunderstanding and she asked me to leave."

Again, he didn't want the answer. "What kind of misunderstanding?"

"I wanted to try something new. She didn't."

Rex left the conversation there. He didn't need specific details about what Bill was doing behind closed doors.

Chapter XI

Your request is denied but it perfectly suits my needs.

My first instinct was survival now that I was here. But I'm carrying the burden of knowing I'm here because I trusted too easily. I was warned to be cautious, I was warned to be careful, I was warned not to trust anyone. But how do you stop trusting someone you've known your whole life? After this, if I survive, I don't know if I'll ever be able to trust another person again.

Aside from the pully system and make-believe window, the room I'm hanging in is nothing but exposed brick and a heavy, metal door that sounded like the entire building would collapse around me if it was slammed too hard. Without the opening and closing of the door, the squeak and grind of the pulley, and the captor's singing, I was left in silence. Alone, with nothing but my thoughts.

Rex brought Bobby in late that afternoon. He asked Randy, Bobby's father, to join them since Bobby was still a minor. Martin also sat in on the questioning. For two hours they went in circles, asking about Beth-Ann and then Sue Ellen. No matter how many times, or how they asked the questions, his answers always remained the same. Most times, if someone is lying, their responses to the questions will change.

"Randy, I appreciate you bringing him in and for allowing us to question him without interruption."

Randy nodded. "I'm not going to pretend I'm happy about it, but you have a job to do. Both you and I have daughters. I know, just as you would, if it were my daughter, I would want everything done correctly if it meant she would come home safe."

Rex gave him one nod to indicate they were on the same page. He sunk into a chair once they walked out the door.

"Well, I guess that's one plus to being in a podunk town like this. I've never seen a father so calm during questioning."

"Randy is a good guy. He also has a daughter, so he understands."

"I'm sure he does. So, what do you think about Bobby? Should we tail him to see where he goes?"

Rex rolled his eyes. "No. I don't think he did it. I think we need to start canvassing again. Now that we have two, we need to check alibis again for every person in town."

Parker finally spoke. "We can divide it up and it'll take half the time."

Martin sighed. "We can divide it up and it'll take one-third of the time. You're going by yourself."

THREE MONTHS LATER

"Walker."

"Kelsey never came home. She promised she would be home by nine, but she never came home. No one has seen her since this afternoon." Suzanne sounded like she was in full panic mode.

"Give me a few minutes. I'll be right over." Rex ended the call and looked at the time. It was only eleven, but he was pulled from a deep sleep. He hadn't been sleeping well, but since the day Beth-Ann disappeared, he got short clips of deep sleep and then stayed awake the rest of the night. He kissed Marilyn's cheek, pulled on a pair of jeans and a T-shirt from his dresser, and headed out. On his drive over, he called Martin and asked him to meet him.

The two other detectives had been in town for over three months and this would be the first time they were here when a girl went missing. Even with help, none of them were having any luck finding witnesses or suspects. These girls were just vanishing without any evidence left behind.

Rex got there before Martin and went inside, wanting to get as much information as soon as possible. Suzanne sat on the couch. Tear streaks stained her face.

"Jim is out in the fields looking for her. He thinks maybe she just needs some time to herself. I should have called you earlier, as soon as I knew she wasn't where she said she was going to be."

"Why don't we start there?" Rex sat in a reclining chair opposite Suzanne. "When is the last time you saw her?"

"I was in the fields most of the day. She asked if she could go out with Bobby since they start school in a couple days. I told her she could. That was during breakfast. I don't know what time she left, but she told me, she promised, she would be home by nine. But then, when I went out to pick up some items from the grocer, I ran into Bobby. He said they didn't have any plans today. I should have called you right then. This is all my fault." She buried her face in her hands. Rex could still see the dirt buried deep under her nails.

"None of this is your fault. We can't keep our kids locked away in the house as much as we may want to. What time did you see Bobby?" Martin knocked and let himself in, sitting on an armchair beside the couch.

"I saw him around four. He told me they didn't have plans and he hadn't spoken to her all day."

"Do you have any idea where she may have gone throughout the day?"

Suzanne shook her head. "You know, I really don't ask. These are all good kids. As long as I know who she's going out with, I don't ask any more questions."

Martin sighed and Rex shot hit an evil look. "Okay. We're going to talk to Bobby now. I know it's late, but please call any friends you think she might be with. And let me know if she does come home, okay? We'll stop by again in the morning."

She thanked them for coming out and closed the door behind them.

"Are you people serious? You now have three missing teenage girls and you don't ask where they're going when they leave the house?"

"First of all, I always ask my daughter where she's going and so does my wife. But yes, most people here do things a little differently. We all know each other, most of us grew up here. We let the kids go because they're teenagers. They have to be allowed to get in trouble sometimes."

"Getting in trouble will get you missing or killed. That's how that goes."

After speaking with Bobby, they went back to the station to add to the information board. The posted Kelsey's picture and all the specifics they received from Suzanne and Bobby. Bobby let Rex check his phone so he could prove they hadn't made any plans. Of course, Rex knew he could have deleted phone calls and messages, but he didn't have enough for a warrant. Bobby's word and willingness to show his phone would have to be enough.

Chapter XII

Your instincts have served you well. You should never fully trust another.

Three weeks after we moved to the new house my curiosity got the better of me. I waited until my mother left for work and crept up the stairs to the forbidden door. Leaning my ear against the wood, I listened for any sign of movement. Even though I watched her leave, I thought, somehow, I might find my mother hiding behind the door, waiting for me to disobey her instructions. A low, constant grinding sound was all I could hear. I turned the knob and cracked the door just enough to see the light spill through. Hesitating a moment more, I pushed the door open and stepped inside. A mobile, unlike any I had seen before, hung from the ceiling in the center of the room.

It moved in a slow rotation, each of my sister's marionettes on full display. I knew it had to be a cruel joke. I stood there for an hour, watching each of the puppets pass in front of me repeatedly;

their limbs loose, but the strings taught. The only one not hanging from the contraption was her favorite, the one she risked it all for. That one stood proudly displayed on top of a dresser. My mother tried to fix it, although I don't know why. A crack ran diagonally across its face, from the hairline to the bottom of its chin. The surface on each side of the crack no longer matched up; one side sunk deeper than the other and fine, spiderwebbed lines now patterned the surface. A glob of clear glue sat along the uneven seam on its forehead where my mother took little care to file it properly.

I fought the urge to reach for the puppet, grab it by its face, and crush it in my fist. Anger rose inside me, turning my muscles to stone and setting my skin to fire. All that time spent building and hanging the marionette mobile, gluing the shattered face of the beloved, trying to fix what was beyond repair. My mother failed with the puppet, just as she failed with my sister. Still, she tried with both and still, she left me wanting.

Rex found Pastor Timothy in his office at the church. The door was open and watched as he wrote some words, scratched them out, and wrote some more, shaking his head. "Pastor?"

He looked up from his desk, visibly distraught. "Sheriff. How can I help you?" He put his pen down and stood.

Rex sighed, wondering what he was doing questioning their pastor. It was a lead he had to follow up on, no matter how uncomfortable it made him. "I have a couple questions I was hoping you might be able to answer."

"I can answer to my ability. Let's walk."

Rex followed him out and waited while Timothy locked the office door behind him. He wondered why in movies and television, and now, in real life, you never saw someone just have a conversation with a clergy member. Scenes were always shown with people walking around the church, never just sitting in one place. "I am here on official business. Any information you can give would really help." Timothy looked at him, nodded, but didn't say a word. "I know you heard that Kelsey Sheridan went missing yesterday."

"It's a tragedy these young women keep disappearing."

It was Rex's turn to nod even though Pastor Timothy wasn't looking at him. "I have a witness who says she saw Kelsey walking to the church yesterday afternoon. Can you tell me if you saw her?"

"She was here. It was early afternoon."

"Her family doesn't frequent the church often. Can you tell me why she was here?"

"Sheriff, you know I'm willing to help you as much as I can, especially for the safety of the girls. But I can't tell you why she stopped by."

He knew these types of answers were coming. Still, he hoped Timothy might give him something he could use. "Can you tell me if she was upset or distraught? Was she in any kind of trouble?"

"I can't answer that either. All I can say is that she was not in any sort of immediate trouble. She stopped by, we talked, and she left."

"Was she by herself?"

"As far as I could tell, yes."

Rex had a lot of respect for their pastor, even so, he could feel his muscles tightening at the lack of forthcoming information. "Did you question that given everything that's been happening?"

"It wasn't my place to ask. Most members come and see me alone."

Without realizing while it was happening, Pastor Timothy had walked Rex to the front door of the church. While he didn't have a good reason to suspect Timothy of any wrongdoing, he would remember the negative gesture. "Thank you for your time, Pastor."

Saturday morning Rex stopped at the hardware store to talk to Colton. Cyrus told him he had gone to Jake's to look at an electrical issue he was having outside. "While I'm here, last Friday, did you happen to see Kelsey going over toward the church? I have a witness saying they saw her heading up that way."

Cyrus frowned and shook his head. "No. I can't see anything from inside here. Plus, I usually work the back of the store and Colton works the front. If I am outside, it's because I'm either coming or going, but I don't pay attention to anything that happens outside the parking lot."

"Have you seen the pastor the past couple days?"

He shook his head again. "We don't really speak other than to exchange pleasantries."

Rex thanked him for his time and drove over to Jake's, hoping to find Colton still there. When he arrived, he found Colton all but wrapped around a light pole at the end of the driveway. He got out of his truck and walked over. "What are you doing?"

"Trying to put this back together. There was a connectivity issue, which I fixed, but now I can't get the top back on." The driveway was long and a set of tall lamp posts lined each side of the driveway.

"Here, let me help you." Rex grabbed the top panel out of his hand and placed it on top of the glass, popping it into place.

"Seriously? I've been working on that for ten minutes."

"Glad I could help. I have a couple questions for you, if you don't mind."

"Don't mind at all." He took a rag from the back pocket of his jeans and wiped the sweat from his forehead.

"Friday, were you working?"

"I sure was. Fridays are always busy." He took a long drink from his water bottle. "I did go over to the post office early afternoon, before the rush."

"Hm. Did you happen to see anyone walking toward the church, or away from it, at any point?"

"Now that you mention it, yeah. On my way back I saw someone going towards it, but I couldn't tell who it was. I thought it was a little odd on a Friday afternoon, but a lot more people have been going for the last few months."

Rex nodded. The church had been full every Sunday since Beth-Ann disappeared and dwindled week by week until the next girl went missing. "I have a witness who says it was Kelsey who was walking over there. Would you be able to confirm that?"

Colton shook his head. "No, like I said, I didn't pay much attention. And they were far away."

Rex had forgotten how large this house was. He almost never came over this far, even when he was out patrolling. He'd never been inside and thought it had looked half-abandoned for years. The only thing it was missing were the boards in the windows.

"Wait a minute. Why are you over here talking to me? Why not just ask the pastor?"

"I did speak to Timothy. But, you know how he is. Even for something like this, he won't break his confidentiality. Martin went and spoke with him first. Hoping that because he knows me, he would give me a little something more, I went to follow-up with him. He did let me look around the church. I didn't find anything. You're the second person to tell me they saw someone go to the building, but no one has mentioned that person leaving."

"You don't think Pastor Timothy has anything to do with all this do you? I've been going to talk to him every week since Beth-Ann disappeared."

"I sure hope he doesn't, but at this point everyone is a suspect and no one is a suspect."

"What about Bobby? Did you talk to him again?" Colton was starting to get antsy. Any time the subject of the girls came up, it made him visibly uncomfortable.

"I've talked to Bobby every time now. I know he has a close connection to all three, but I'm wondering why everyone is so quick to try to blame him. He's never had a bad reputation."

"I can't say when it comes to Sue Ellen, but two of the three are his girlfriend and his ex-girlfriend. I never had a problem with the kid, but seriously, who's next? His sister?" He shook his head and Rex could see he was getting upset. "I've got to get back to the store." Without another word, he got in his vehicle and drove off, leaving Rex alone in the driveway.

Chapter XIII

Perfection. Everyone is playing their role, even those without any lines.

Every day was the same as the last. He would come in and do my makeup and change my dress. Before putting the new one on, he would stare just a little too long. After what I could only assume had been months, it never got any more comfortable. I could feel his eyes searing into my skin, thinking about how I feel and how I taste. Every two days my undergarments were changed and every time, it brought a new type of torment with it. The changing rituals of those garments meant the slow caress of hands down my body, followed by a lingering trail of kisses and gentle, slow flicks of his tongue, strategically placed. No matter how many times it happened, it sent a cold chill through my body.

Each string had a metal hook and loop attached to the top for easy removal and replacement of my clothing. Sundays, he told me were laundry days, and all my clothing was removed in its entirety. I was positioned and posed the way I came into the word, fully exposed. My positioning was different every day and each seemed to be worse than the last. I was weak and underfed. My muscles hurt and my wrists, ankles, arms, and legs were all rubbed raw from the strings pulling and being wrapped so tight. I was scared, lonely, and confused. I had to wonder if the other girls were here, too. I had to wonder if they were being treated the same way.

Maris sat at the counter of the bakery. She stopped by once a week to satisfy her sweet tooth. As much as she loved to cook and bake, she refused to do so if it were only for herself. She watched Sally as she wiped down the center island and counters that were not for customer use. "Why don't you take a break? Come sit with me for a few minutes?"

"You know, I think I might. Let me get myself a cup of coffee and I'll come chat with you. I could use a distraction of sorts." She washed her hands in the over-sized sink, perfect for washing large pans, poured herself a mug of dark roast coffee and plated a chocolate muffin. She made her way to the outside of the counter and sat two stools away from Maris.

"Well, I'm glad you're willing to get off your feet for a few minutes, but I'm not sure I like the idea of being a distraction." She grinned at Sally and patted her hand. "How are you doing?"

Sally's eyes floated toward the countertop and she shrugged. "It's just hard. I don't have any daughters to worry about, so that's good. And Rex keeps telling me that Roy isn't a suspect, but I still can't help wondering what's really going on in his head. Does he look at Roy differently now than he did a few months ago? Is he looking at Walt and I in a new way, thinking we raised some kind of terrible child?" She shook her head. She hadn't made eye contact with Maris once since she sat down. Her eyes began to water and she was thankful it had been quiet in the bakery the past few days. She would hate to have her customers see her cry. Maris was different, she was like Sally's own mother. She wiped her hand under one eye. "And Roy. My baby. He's having such a hard time. Do you know what it's like to see an almost grown man walk around in a daze almost every day? At this point, I don't even think he's upset anymore. I think he's just numb. The police have questioned him twice, his girlfriend and friends are still missing, and his best friend is the prime suspect. It is so hard to watch him struggle and not be able to help him. No words will make what he's going through easier." One tear was making its way down her face, but she didn't bother to wipe it away.

"I can't say I know what it's like to see your child suffer, but I do know he's a strong person. And you raised him well. He's respectful and kind and I know he'll pull through this. Just like all the rest of us will. Regardless of which side a person is on, every Dunmeyer resident is suffering right now in their own way. We'll get through this together, as a community. We just have to keep supporting each other." She reached over and plucked the Hershey's kiss off the top of Sally's untouched muffin and popped it in her mouth.

Sally let out a hearty laugh. "Well, I was going to eat that."

"You've got plenty." Maris smiled as wide as she could, thankful her little quirks were able to make so many people happy. "Besides, I only ordered a bran muffin. You have a muffin full of chocolate. I needed it more than you."

"Maris, thank you for being you. I don't think any of us would make it through a day without you." As did most of the town, June loved Maris wholeheartedly. She couldn't imagine what it would be like if Maris weren't here.

"Why don't you all come to my place for dinner tomorrow night? It'll be nice for you to have a night away from cooking. You can bring dessert."

"We would like that. Thank you."

The meal laid out in front of them was incredible. Maris always went through so much trouble when she invited people over for dinner. Sally felt uncomfortable knowing how much effort she put in, but she knew how much Maris loved doing it. Without having a family of her own, it made Maris feel good to be able to put on such an elaborate meal. Rather than a casual, get-together meal of lasagna or a casserole, Maris put on ham, potatoes, mixed vegetables, gravy, and rolls. She arranged her table with fine china, a matching set down to the trays, pitcher, and gravy boat, and a beautiful centerpiece with sunflowers, lilies, and greens. Even the two men smiled when they saw it.

"Maris. You always go through so much trouble. It's just us." Sally tried not to sound put off by the display. "This table is beautiful. It looks like an ad in a magazine."

Maris gently slapped the back of Sally's arm. "You know it's no trouble at all. I love preparing meals and setting the table. I even enjoy the clean up afterward."

Sally shook her head and smiled. "I brought a bundt cake for dessert. I hope lemon is okay?"

"It is as long as you guys don't mind if you don't get any." Maris retrieved the platter from Sally's hands and sashayed her way into the kitchen. Sally, to this day, had no idea how Maris had managed to stay single. She was so spunky one couldn't help but smile whenever she was around. Maris emerged from the kitchen with a bottle of wine in one hand and a glass of iced tea in the other. She handed the bottle to Walt and set the glass in front of Roy. "Dig in everyone. This food isn't going to eat itself."

They passed plates around the table to make sure they all got a helping of each dish. It felt strange to the Carlsons. They typically did a grab and run with both lunch and dinner. Walt and Roy would find a game to watch on tv and Sally would read a book. It wasn't ideal for every family, but it worked for them. The only time they had a real, sit-down meal was on a holiday or if they were guests in someone else's home.

They talked about Roy's plans for college, some gossip about people in town, and the upcoming annual carnival. When they finished eating, Maris stood and started stacking plates. "Roy, why don't you help me clear the table and we'll get some coffee going for dessert."

They stacked the dishes on the counter and Maris bustled about the kitchen starting the coffee pot and grabbing mugs and plates for everyone while Roy cut into the cake. "Now, Roy. I know you probably don't want to confide in an old bat like me, but I can see you're trying hard to keep up appearances. How are you really doing?" He set the knife down and turned to her. She could see the hurt and confusion in his eyes.

"You're not an old bat. Truth is, it's been a hard couple of months. I know people are scared and I understand the concern, but I can't go anywhere without people staring at me and whispering when they think I can't hear them. We're supposed to be a community, we're supposed to support each other. My parents feel isolated, like people are looking at them differently, and Bobby said the same about his family. Of course, I'm worried about the girls, we have no idea if they're even still alive now. But I can handle people thinking poorly of me, I know I didn't do anything wrong. I don't like the way they're treating my best friend and our families. That's the worst part for me."

Maris reached up as far as she could, standing on her toes, and put her hand on Roy's shoulder. "There are a lot of us that know you didn't do anything. We also don't blame either of your families for what's happening. The important thing is to keep going with your daily life. Do not let other's opinions bring you down. You're right, people are scared and they want someone to blame. Your friends happened to be the target of a very serious crime. Because you're connected to the girls, in the minds of ignorant people, that means you're also connected to the crime. And Sheriff Walker, well, he might as well have taken the girls himself." She shook her head and stared at the floor. "You saw how fast everyone turned on him at the town meeting. He's one of the most respected men in our town and people were out for blood that night."

"You're right. It's just so hard to watch everything that's happening and not have any control or any way to fix it." His face contorted and Maris could see him straining to keep his composure behind watery eyes.

"If you ever need to talk, I'm always around. You can stop by any time." She saw him nod and knew the conversation had run its course. "Let's get this coffee and cake out to your parents before they think we got lost."

They filled two serving trays, one with steaming mugs of coffee and one with plates of lemon cake. "Maris? Thank you."

She patted the top of his hand and said nothing more.

Chapter XIV

Cut. It's wrong. It's all wrong.

I used to love exploring the woods in our neighborhood. It gave me a sense of peace I couldn't find at home. I chose to spend time outside, listening to birds chirping, twigs snapping beneath my feet, rather than cruising around with other kids my age. I felt safe there. Being in the woods was the one place I could be alone without feeling lonely. The trees were densely packed and someone could easily get lost if they didn't know the way. I had a favorite spot, one I would visit multiple times a week, with a tree that loomed larger then the rest. It had a small clearing around it as if it commanded more room, more space to call its own, and the afternoon sun hit it exactly right, so the ground appeared to glow.

When I left after graduation, I didn't miss the town, the people, my mother; I missed coming to this spot. I missed letting the hours melt away while I leaned against the tree reading, doing homework, or daydreaming about a better life. Finding this place of solitude, a space to call my own, allowed me to refocus and set my life on track for a better future. I left town for six years before coming back to live with my mother. I thought going to school and earning a degree would make her see that I had worth, that I wasn't as useless as she believed. I thought it would make her finally see me as a person. I was wrong.

Being back in this cold, empty house was worse than it had ever been. I remembered the promise I made to myself when I was young, after I broke my sister's puppet. I remembered telling myself I would get my revenge somehow. I finally have that chance. If she doesn't want to see what I have to offer, what I'm capable of, I'll force her to see it. After a lifetime of abuse and neglect, it's time for me to fulfill that promise. The time for my revenge is now.

She didn't put up much of a fight. I thought she would try a little harder, but I had become used to the disappointment. I should have known she would let me down one last time. I spent a week, leading up to this moment, planning everything. I chose the perfect spot for her, the place that brought me peace when I was a teenager, that large tree that stood all by itself. I needed a marker and, despite her making me feel alone my entire life, I wanted her to have something to take with her. I set out with two large thermoses of water, a pair of gloves, a large pocketknife, and a chisel. I cleared the space around the base of the tree, so I wouldn't be kneeling on sticks or rocks, and began chipping away at the bark.

I started with the face, carving the outline with my knife and using the chisel for the more delicate features. The cross brace on top came out crooked and sat at an odd angle. Piece by piece, I carved out the body and each limb. The proportions were horrendous, but I was never a great art student. I stepped back, sweating, and swiped my forehead with the back of my hand. Aside from the face, to anyone who saw this carving, it would look like a jumbled mess, but I knew what it stood for. This symbol marked my freedom. It gave me hope for the future, a reason to keep going.

I promised my mother I would take care of my sister. Her eyes pleaded with me, but she said nothing. I stood over her, watching the life drain from her body. As she took her last breath, I finally felt the freedom I had longed for all those years. I always believed it was attention I was seeking, validation and reassurance. It was none of those things. What I needed was mental freedom knowing I was no longer under her scrutiny. With her lying there, eyes still staring up at me, I felt the euphoria wash over my body.

It took me days to dispose of her properly. I left her in the bathtub while I went to the woods to dig a hole. I was careful, digging deeper than a person usually would. I didn't want someone to catch me; I couldn't risk having my freedom stripped away as soon as I'd acquired it. I put my mother in her favorite dress, a last-minute gesture to tell her there were no hard feelings. After dropping her in the hole and filling it in, I packed the dirt with the back of the shovel, ridding myself of the rest of the anger flowing through my veins.

I went home and took a long, scalding shower. I scrubbed the dirt from my skin, my hair, and under my nails. The initial heat eased the tension in my muscles, but I stood there until the water ran cold because there was no longer anyone there to stop me. I toweled off and dressed in a pair of flannel pants and a t-shirt before settling on the couch. I should have made something for my sister to eat for dinner, but it was too late. She was sleeping peacefully.

Bobby jerked the wheel of his truck and slammed on the brakes just off the side of the road.

Sarah's body flew forward and she grabbed the dashboard for support. "What was that for?"

Bobby twisted around and stared at her. "What is your problem, Sarah? For the last week you've given me nothing but attitude. Even mom asked what I did to you."

Her eyes, filled with tears, met his. Her voice was weak and strained. "I'm sorry. I just...did you do it Bobby? Did you make all those girls disappear?"

"I don't believe this." He slammed the heel of his hand into the steering wheel and threw his door open, his face red with anger. "My own sister."

Sarah followed him out of the truck. She hadn't seen him this angry in a long time. "I just need to know. It doesn't matter what the answer is, I just need to know the truth."

Bobby had his back against the truck bed. He opened his mouth to speak but paused as Clint pulled his truck over behind him. Jimmy stuck his arm out the passenger window in greeting.

As the two exited the truck, Bobby refocused on the conversation with his sister. He shouted at her. "You're right. My answer doesn't matter because the people who are supposed to have my back, the people who are supposed to be supporting me don't even trust me. It doesn't matter what I say."

"Bobby..."

"No, Sarah. Don't try to pretend now. The simple fact that you felt the need to ask that question tells me everything I need to know."

"I just wanted the truth. I thought maybe if you had something to share, you'd be more comfortable telling me. I thought you would have enough trust in me."

"Why? Because you have so much trust in me? I have been telling the truth, right from the beginning."

Sarah and Bobby stared at each other, not knowing what else to say. Clint stepped between them. "Everything okay here?"

"Fine." Bobby turned his back and hoisted himself into his truck. "Give Sarah a ride home for me?" He didn't wait for an answer before spinning his tires and driving away.

Jimmy was leaning against his brother's truck, arms crossed, unsure of what to do. Sarah had tears streaming down her face and Clint walked over and wrapped his arms around her. "I'm not sure what just happened, but I'll bring you home whenever you're ready."

Two hours later, Bobby walked through the front door and into the kitchen. His mother was standing at the stove, stirring a pot of pasta sauce. The sun was shining directly through the kitchen window above the sink, illuminating the side of her face. Bobby walked up behind her, set his hands on her shoulders, and kissed her cheek. "Hi, mom. Dinner smells great."

"Thank, honey. It'll be ready in about five minutes." She turned and scanned the kitchen. "Where's your sister?"

Bobby's heart sunk and his voice caught in his throat. "She's not here?"

"Bobby." She sounded exasperated. "Please tell me you didn't forget her?"

His heart pounded so hard he could hear it in his ears. "Of course not. Besides, she would have called. Clint was going to bring her the rest of the way home."

"Go call her phone, right now." Her voice was just shy of a yell and he didn't blame her. "And what do you mean, 'the rest of the way home'?"

He raised his finger to tell her to give him a minute. The phone rang for the second time as the front door opened and Sarah stepped in. Bobby breathed a sigh of relief and his mother pushed by him, practically running to his sister. She wrapped her arms around her daughter.

"I'm so glad you're home. Your brother just about gave me a heart attack when he said you weren't with him." She eased her grip and pushed Sarah to arm's length, tears welling in her eyes. "Next time you aren't with the person you're supposed to be with, please send me a message. We're all on edge right now and we can never be too safe."

"Okay, mom. Sorry. I didn't think it was that big of a deal. I was with Clint and Jimmy, you know them." Sarah's top lip curled. She didn't understand the problem. She hung out with them all the time.

"Yes, Sarah, I do. But I didn't know you were with them. I thought you were with your brother. He came home without you and my mind immediately went into full panic mode." She loosened her grip on Sarah's shoulders. "We can't take any chances with everything that's happening right now. Honestly, you're lucky we're even letting you out of the house."

Sarah rolled her eyes. "I get it, mom. I said I was sorry. I'll let you know next time. But, to be fair, maybe you should be talking to Bobby since he's the one who left me." There was a defiance in her voice as she shot Bobby an angry look.

June closed her eyes and took a deep breath. Walking back to the kitchen she glared at Bobby and pointed her finger at him. "We'll talk later." Her voice was stern and Bobby knew he would be lucky to see the light of day for the next few weeks.

Everyone in the Chambers' household had gone to their rooms. June and Randy were lying in bed, talking about what they could do better to keep their kids safe. Bobby was listening to music, staring at the ceiling, trying to figure out how he could prove to everyone that he was innocent. Sarah was sitting on the edge of her bed, biding her time before she could leave. She knew she had to give everyone at least an hour before they drifted off. One perk of having the only bedroom on the ground floor was that she was able to sneak out her window easily without anyone finding out. It had become a weekend tradition for her, mainly just for fun, but tonight, she needed to get out. She needed fresh air to clear her head. She didn't have any plans or anyone to meet up with. She just wanted to go for a walk to sort out her thoughts. She was so angry with Bobby for leaving her earlier, she was upset that she doubted him about telling the truth, and now she didn't think her parents would ever let her out of the house again without a chaperone.

She spent the next hour and fifteen minutes mindlessly scrolling through social media apps on her phone. Once she was sure everyone had fallen asleep, she pulled her sneakers on and carefully opened her window. As she had done at least a couple dozen times before, she sat on the edge of the sill, swung both legs out, flipped over onto the stomach and slithered down the other side so she landed quietly on the grass. Stepping on to the rocks that lined the edge of the house, she slid the window closed before jogging to the edge of her yard and down the side of the driveway. The trees that lined their property provided plenty of coverage for her to get away from the house unseen. Once she hit the road, she was free.

After how warm it had been during the day, she didn't expect the air to be as cold as it was. She was so focused on being able to get out, she hadn't thought of bringing a sweater. She wore jeans and a tank top and after being outside for thirty minutes goosebumps prickled her skin and the chill went deep to her bones. She stopped walking for a moment and closed her eyes, inhaling deep breaths of the crisp air. Despite the cold, she needed this time to herself to clear her head. Not wanting to push how long she was gone, she decided to make her way back. As soon as she turned, she heard the rumble of the car and saw headlights in the distance. She wondered, besides herself, who would be out so late. It was after midnight when she left her room and it was a weekday.

She started her trek back home and as the car got closer, her heart rate sped up. She hadn't given much thought to what was happening in their town apart from what Bobby was going through. Being out in the open, in the middle of the night, by herself wasn't something she had taken into consideration until she saw someone else out. Her nerves got the better of her and she started shaking. She sidestepped into the narrow cover of a small stretch of trees that lined the road. She felt safer in the shadows, until the car slowed and stopped right beside her.

Chapter XV

The beauty. The innocence. A complement to the rest.

When I awoke, I couldn't open my eyes. I felt as if I had exhausted every part of my body, my eyelids felt weighted down. I tried to struggle against the hands I could feel running down the length of me. My attempts proved to be futile. My head felt fuzzy and I couldn't tell if he had me lying down or pinned against a wall. The cold, hard surface my back brushed against scratched at my skin. My captor had removed most of my clothing and his hands made their way over every inch of exposed flesh. My skin prickled and the hair stood up over my entire body. He leaned forward and whispered in my ear.

"Didn't your parents ever teach you not to be so trusting? No matter how well you think you know someone, you never truly know them." He ran his tongue from the top of my shoulder to my earlobe and I cringed beneath his touch. "Mmm.

I'm going to have so much fun with you. So young, so... innocent."

His hands wrapped around my waist and pulled me forward, letting me know he had me leaning against a wall. I felt something tug at my arms and whimpered at the pain of my shoulders and hands feeling like they were ripping away from my body. I still couldn't open my eyes, but my mind began to clear. Suspended in the air, my body swung gently back and forth. I used every ounce of energy I could muster to move away from the feeling of my captor's tongue grazing the inside of my thigh. I was still too weak to stop it.

Colton had just opened the store when Rex stormed in. "Morning, sheriff. You're out early."

"Not by choice. We need to talk." His answer was short and his tone told Colton he wasn't in the mood to entertain small talk.

"Sure. We can talk in my office." He led the way to the back and waited for Rex to sit before closing the door behind them. "It sounds serious. Do you have news about Beth-Ann?" He sat behind the desk, bracing himself for the worst.

"I'm sorry, but I don't have any news. I do need to know where you were last night, though." He tried to keep a neutral expression on his face, but he could feel his jaw tensing and his brow furrowing.

"Geez, you make it sound like I'm a suspect or something. What happened?"

"Just answer the question."

"I was home, with Kimberley. Why do you need to know?" His response came out in a staccato. He wasn't happy.

"Sarah's gone. And the last time I talked to you, you asked if she was next."

Colton pushed his chair back and jumped off the seat. "Are you kidding me? I was talking about Bobby and how close he was to the other girls. Why the fuck would I kidnap a child when mine was the first to disappear? I know the heartbreak. I know how hard it is to watch your own family become numb and emotionless. For five months Kimberley and I have been worried and wondering and hoping, but we're not living. We're just going through the motions because we have two other children we need to worry about. You knew exactly what I was talking about when I made that comment." His face was red and spit flew out of his mouth as he yelled. "If you're not here to arrest me, get the fuck out of my office."

Rex felt isolated from almost everyone in the community that he swore to protect. Frank hadn't willingly spoken to him in months. Pastor Timothy had quietly shown him the door, and Kimberley, Ely, and Emily wouldn't give him so much as a courtesy nod when they saw him in public. Now, Colton, who was one of his closest friends, had sent him away and Rex didn't know if he would ever forgive him after this case was closed. He didn't blame him and wondered of he would have done the same if the roles were reversed.

He drove aimlessly around town. It was a new habit he had picked up over the last few months. Driving always had a calming effect on him, but he used it as more of a distraction now. With every ounce of his being he wanted to drive away, keep going past the town's boundaries, past the state line, and just disappear himself for a few weeks. Maybe if he did, he would drive back and realize everything he was going through was nothing more than a nightmare.

He knew all too well it was a nightmare, but he was awake and he was living in it. Driving off wouldn't help to find the girls and it wouldn't rid him of any guilt he was feeling about not being able to find them. He pulled himself back to reality and saw the flag he had posted on the side of the road by the tree with the face. He pulled over and took the walk through the woods. Maybe the face would distract him from his current mindset. Months after he had first been introduced, he still couldn't figure out the significance.

Chapter XVI

My pride and joy. The object of my desire. I shall cast the final roll.

I watched this one every day. She was my desire, my dream. Her dress, handmade, laid out for months already, waited for me to mold it to her body. She would become the perfect marionette, the replica of the broken puppet that caused my sister's dive out the second story window. She would be the one to make my collection complete. Her look was different from the others, flawless skin, black hair, petite. She was so perfect. I followed her to school in the mornings, watched her swim at the pool on the weekends, wash in the shower afterward. I practiced her makeup on the other girls to be sure I could do it just right. There was no room for error when it came to my star. Lizbeth Walker would become my Geisha marionette. She would make all my dreams come true.

After school, Lizbeth made her way to the pool as she did every Wednesday. None of her friends enjoyed swimming like she did, so she went by herself. It gave her time to clear her head and, being alone, she could take as much or as little time as she wanted. She went into the locker room, changed into her bathing suit, and piled her hair in a bun. She pulled her swim cap over her head, not the most fashion-forward of looks, but it saved her from having to wash the chlorine out of her hair.

She needed the swim today. Her mind was reeling from thinking about grades, college, and her missing friends. She didn't plan to stay as long as she did. Once she got into the pool, she could feel the stress leaving her body and she didn't want to go home. He didn't do it on purpose, but just seeing her father made her friend's disappearance real. She saw the stress and worry on his face, the toll it was taking on him mentally. She took a quick break, promised herself ten more laps and she would head home. She pushed off and immediately felt better again. She stuck to her own word and pulled herself out of the pool after her tenth lap. She changed back into her clothes, pulled off her swim cap, and packed her suit. As soon as she stepped outside, a loud rumble of thunder sounded and the skies opened up. Huge drops of rain crashed on the pavement around her feet. She looked up at the sky in every direction and realized the rain wasn't going to go away any time soon. It was only a fifteen minute walk from the pool to her house, but in a downpour, the walk was not ideal.

She made it two streets down the main road before she cut off onto a small side street that would chop a few minutes off her travel time. A car sped past her, slowed, and pulled to the side. She hesitated, but only for a moment. She recognized the driver as they opened the door and got out. They waved. "Lizbeth? Let me give you a ride home. It's pouring out here."

Lizbeth was freezing and dripping wet. She couldn't say 'no' when she had barely begun her journey home. She jogged to the car. "Thank you so much. I know it's supposed to be fall but the rain is so cold." She sat on the passenger seat and dropped her bag between her feet. She rubbed her hands together to warm them up. And then she felt it, the sharp pinch in her arm.

"Don't worry, honey. You'll wake up in a few hours."

Those were the last words she heard before her head fell to the side and her vision went black.

Rex felt like he couldn't breathe. His vision went dark around the edges and he had to sit down. Marilyn just called him in a panic, telling him Lizbeth hadn't come home yet. He always knew it was a possibility, but he had to believe it couldn't, or wouldn't happen to them. He prided himself on being able to separate his work life from his home life, but at times like this it was hard to do. He took a few cleansing breaths to lower his heart rate and clear his head. "Martin."

"Yeah?"

"I need you to take me home. My daughter is missing. You need to take a statement from my wife"

Martin opened his mouth to speak, shut it again, and then replied. "Oh, no. Do you think it's the same person or did you just piss off the wrong person this time?"

"I don't know. I've made so many enemies since this all started. It could be revenge, it could be the same kidnapper, maybe she's just hurt and is running late." He stood slowly and started towards the door. "She swims a couple times a week. Let's stop at the pool on the way to my house."

They left Parker on his own to canvass all the local businesses to see if he could spot her anywhere. They stopped at the pool and then went straight to Rex's home. Marilyn fell into his arms the moment he came through the door. He tried so hard to remain still and not run out the door to look for Lizbeth. He had to stop himself multiple times from interrupting the interview and asking questions. He was lucky Martin let him stay in the room. He held Marilyn's hand as she dabbed at her eyes with the other.

When Martin finished taking her statement, Rex was torn with what to do. He wanted to stay home and try to comfort Marilyn. He also needed to feel her presence for his own comfort. But he was itching to get out. He had felt helpless for so many months, he didn't think it could get any worse. He was wrong. He had never felt so hopeless, useless, or helpless in his life. He needed to do something to make himself feel like he was doing some good in trying to find Lizbeth. His mind was pulling him in every different direction.

"I'm going to go back to the station with Martin. I'll pick up my truck and then I'm going to drive around a bit to see if I can find her anywhere. I'll call you later, okay? And please call me if she comes home."

"Be careful." She hugged him and watched him until they turned out of the driveway.

CURRENT
DAY

Rex was numb. He couldn't tell how he was feeling anymore. He spent the first few hours of the day staring at a wall at the station. When Bobby came in, he was mean to him, and completely dismissed everything he had to say. Martin and Parker were getting on his last nerve and he was debating calling his old captain and asking him to take them off the case. Finding the letter in his mailbox about Beth-Ann sent his nerves into overdrive. And having to deal with Ruth and her attitude made him so angry. He felt like he was shutting down. Mentally and emotionally, he couldn't take anymore.

He was halfway through the parking lot of the hotel when his phone rang. "Walker."

"It's Martin. We have a fire."

"Where?" Rex stepped up his speed to a slow run.

"The big house on Maple. The one with the shed in the back."

"You on your way?"

"Heading over. We're about halfway there."

"I'll meet you there."

Chapter XVII

The final curtain call. My masterpiece has ended in destruction.

This is it. This is the last day before I prove to everyone how much better I am than my sister. I've spent years perfecting my art, honing my make-up skills, sewing just the right costumes. Tomorrow, I'll dress them all, make up their faces, and move them one by one, down the hall, into the room dedicated as the main stage area. The pedestals are lined up, the ropes are in place, I've adjusted the spotlights and tested the sound system. Once I get the girls in place, I'll be able to control all five at once, three more than my sister ever could. Her puppets all came with dresses and makeup, the strings already attached. I have controlled it all with my puppets. I am their costume designer, their makeup artist, their master puppeteer. My sister, she could control the puppet's movements, but I control their look, their style, their movements, and their thoughts...because I'm better than she ever was.

Tomorrow is a special day. Not only because the stage is set for the greatest performance ever, but it's also Lizbeth's birthday. The big one-eight. I can't wait until then.

Rex was the first emergency responder to arrive. He parked his truck on the side of the road to allow Frank plenty of room to maneuver the fire truck into the driveway. Smoke clouds were rising above the tree tops and Rex could see the flames emerging from the blown out windows, grasping for more oxygen.

He didn't realize how chilly the air had become until he moved closer to the house. The heat from the fire made his skin damp and the cool breeze at his back sent a shiver through his body. He hugged his chest as he called out to listen for any response from inside the house. There were no cars in the driveway, but that didn't mean someone couldn't still be here. He made his way around to the side of the house while maintaining a safe distance and strained to hear any human voices. He called out again but was met only with the screaming siren of the approaching fire engine and the crackling and collapsing of beams. He had responded to a number of fires over the years but was still taken aback every time by how much noise they made.

Martin cupped his hands to the side of his mouth as he approached Rex from behind and called out to him. "Rex." He called louder, "Rex." Rex stopped walking and turned around to face him. Martin beckoned him over with his hand. "Frank just pulled up. The house empty?"

"Seems to be. Resident lives alone and their car isn't here." Rex was yelling to be heard over the miniature explosions taking place beside him.

Frank came rushing past both of them, fire hose in hand. "Move, move, move," he demanded.

Both men stepped to the side. Most would chock his commands up to the severity of the situation, but Rex knew better. He had known Frank since he was young and this was just part of his personality. Frank was cocky and arrogant and he had the "man-in-uniform" cliché working for him but his social skills were severely lacking and it was rare that anyone was able to pull even the slightest amount of common courtesy out of him. He had the type of attitude you would expect from someone with money in a big city, not from a small town fireman who had only left the town limits twice in his entire life.

Martin and Rex made their way back to the front of the house to catch up with Parker. As soon as they got there, they heard Frank yell from the side of the house. "What the hell?" they all asked in unison. Each of them ran back to where they had just come from except Parker who ran around the other side of the house. They heard Frank yell again but couldn't hear what he was saying.

"What? We can't hear you."

"Get. Him. Out of here." He yelled much louder this time and pointed toward the back of the house.

They couldn't see anyone but walked toward the back yard. When they rounded the corner, they could just make out a shadow sliding along the front of the shed. "Stop," Rex shouted. "Don't move." They both saw the shadow stop moving but couldn't see the person it belonged to. They drew their guns at the same time and moved forward cautiously.

Rex heard a familiar voice call out from the darkness. "Don't shoot. I'm right here."

"Bobby?"

"Yeah, it's me. Hey, sheriff."

It was still hard to hear but he sounded more like a mischievous fourteen-year-old than a senior in high school that was a suspected kidnapper. "Bobby. What in the hell are you doing here? I thought I told you to go to school and then home hours ago?"

"You did. And I did go home. And then I came out again."

Just as he finished speaking, Parker stepped into a pool of light, lit by the moon, to let Martin and Rex know he was there. Without any warning, he sprinted toward Bobby and tackled him to the ground from behind.

Rex raced towards them and caught Bobby's right arm just before he managed to hit Parker. He had already used his strength and size to manipulate the situation and Parker's size only served to make it easier for him to do so. "Bobby, stop. He didn't know it was you."

Martin helped Parker to his feet and Rex did the same for Bobby. "Now tell me, what are you doing here?"

Bobby was busy picking leaves out of his hair while he answered. "You weren't listening to me. I had to find a way to make you listen."

Now he sounded like his smart-ass self. It took Rex a minute to process what he was saying. His eyes grew wide and he could feel his heart rate speed up.

"Are you telling me there are people in the house?"

Parker, in his usual fashion, had a complete disregard for the safety of others and was more concerned with slapping a pair of handcuffs on Bobby's wrists. "Bobby Chambers, you're under arrest for arson."

"Christ, Parker. Go put him in the car and get back here and help us." Martin, for the first time, showed true annoyance at his partner.

Rex ran around the side of the house to tell Frank what he just learned. He saw that their local volunteers had shown up and surprisingly, they had most of the fire under control. He relayed his message and went out front to talk to Bobby to see if he could get some information as to exactly where he thought the girls were.

He could see him sitting in the back seat of the patrol car. He looked so innocent sitting there. Rex was having a hard time believing that he had just deliberately set this fire for the purpose of forcing the sheriff to listen to him. He's still a child, but Rex just couldn't understand what would make him do such a thing. In an attempt to potentially save the girls, he may have killed them all. Rex was using every ounce of energy he had left to contain himself from running straight into the burning house.

He approached the car and ripped the back door open. "Get out. What makes you think they're in there?"

Bobby stared at him for a moment. He had been so calm just a few minutes before he couldn't believe the intensity in his voice now. He kicked his feet to the side and scooted to the edge of the seat so he could stand up without falling out of the car. "I've been snooping around, looking in windows for months. This place makes sense."

"What the hell were you thinking? And where do you think they are?" He took a deep breath, but it didn't help to ease the tension in his muscles at all. "I swear to god, Bobby, if she dies in there because of you, I'll kill you myself." He took a step toward him but thought better of it and backed away.

Bobby smiled. "Relax, sheriff. They're fine. I think." He muttered the last statement under his breath and backed into the car when Rex stepped towards him again. "Whoa, whoa. They're fine, I promise. There's a long curtain on the back wall of the kitchen pantry. It looks like it's there for aesthetic purposes but there is actually a heavy, metal door behind it. I think the girls are behind that door."

Rex growled in frustration. "You think? You think, Bobby? Setting that fire was the stupidest thing you could possibly have done. You better hope, if they are in there, that none of them die because of that fire. You could be facing murder charges. You could be going to prison for life." He was yelling but he had no control over his voice. He was scared and frustrated and he felt helpless.

Bobby's mouth was hanging open and he was beginning to shake. He hadn't thought about the consequences of that. He had never set a fire outside of the fire pit before; he didn't expect it to spread so fast once it got going.

"Nothing?"

"I...I don't know what to say. I didn't think about that." His eyes began to well up with tears. "I was only trying to help. I just wanted you to listen to me. I wanted you to take me seriously." He sank back into the patrol car and hung his head.

"You better hope they're all okay or every single person in this town is going to take you very seriously...as an adult...for murder charges." He almost slammed the door closed but remembered at the last second that Bobby's legs were still sticking out. "Get back in the car."

He slammed the door so hard that the entire patrol car shook. He closed his eyes and tried to talk himself into calming down before he went back to talk to Parker and Martin. Martin he would be able to deal with but Parker? He was worried that he may pick him up and throw him in the fire if he said something stupid.

He waited close to two full minutes before he took his first step. When he rounded the corner of the house, he saw all the men standing around talking. He had forgotten how chilly it was outside until he got close to the house again. Even though the fire appeared to be out, the amount of heat still radiating from the house was unsettling to him.

"Bobby said there is a metal door on the back wall of the kitchen pantry. He thinks that's where the girls are."

Frank scrunched up his face. "Metal? That makes a lot of sense since this house is a hundred years old. Everything in this house, with the exception of the appliances, is wood."

The other men chuckled and it made Rex even more furious than he already was. "Will you please just humor me and go look? It's not going to hurt."

Frank sighed and stepped over the threshold that used to be the side of the house. He turned on his flashlight and waved it around what was left of the kitchen. After about thirty seconds they heard him call out. "He's right. There is a huge, metal door in here." He banged on it with the side of his fist and it let out an angry, rumbling growl. Frank sprinted back outside having not taken the integrity of the structure of the house into consideration.

Just when they got clearance from Frank to enter the house, they saw the headlights of a car turning into the driveway. They all paused mid-stride. They were all so caught up with the fire and the idea that the girls may be here, they had temporarily forgotten that the owner of the house may come home and that they were the potential suspected kidnapper that had been terrorizing the town for the past six months.

Rex and Martin approached the vehicle cautiously as it came to a stop. They were expecting a lot of questions. Instead, the driver jumped out of the car without turning off the engine. He ran straight between the two detectives while shouting "My puppets, my puppets" over and over again. He was visibly distraught over his collection.

Martin caught up with the driver just as they reached for the front door handle. "Whoa! Not so fast. It's not safe for you to go in there." He had one hand resting on his opposite side and the other on his shoulder in an attempt to turn him around.

"My puppet collection is in there." He tried to reverse direction again but Martin was stronger than he looked.

"You can't go in there for puppets." Martin rolled his eyes. "It's not safe." He knew stress could make people do strange things, but he couldn't believe someone would risk their life for puppets and there was no way he was going to let someone enter a freshly burned house to try and save a couple of dolls, regardless of how valuable they thought the toys were. *And what kind of adult collects dolls?*

Bobby was still sitting in the back of the patrol car, but he was now thrashing around the back seat and yelling incoherently. He had been perfectly calm and subordinate until a few minutes ago. Now, he was acting more like someone they would be picking up at the bar for a drunk and disorderly.

Against his better judgment but seeing that Martin was busy and knowing that Parker is an idiot, Rex made his way over to the patrol car again and wrenched open the door. "What is the problem, Bobby? We're a little busy here at the moment, in case you didn't know."

"You need him to open the door. Did you find the door? He has the code for you to get the girls."

Rex was standing in the opening of the car door to keep Bobby from jumping out. The messages collided in his mind all at once and he backed up out of the way. "Move your feet." Without waiting to make sure Bobby was clear of the door, he slammed it shut and ran over to Martin, who was still arguing over the puppet collection.

"Puppets," Rex yelled out. "You're talking about the girls, aren't you? You created your own, real life, puppet collection with the girls you kidnapped, the girls who trusted you?" It was a good thing they still needed the code, otherwise Rex was worried he probably would have shot the perp right then.

"Well. We seem to have an intelligent one here. I'm impressed, Rex." His demeanor had changed drastically once Rex called him out. He had been trying to play dumb until this point and pretend he was talking about an actual toy collection to see if he could get Martin to believe him.

"It's sheriff. And the only thing I need you to tell me right now is where the girls are. What's the code to that door?" Rex could almost feel his blood begin to boil. He was already angry but the idea that their perp now thought they were playing a game wasn't sitting right with him. To his surprise, it didn't take much convincing to get the code, but their kidnapper insisted on being the one to enter it. Not willing and lacking the energy to argue anymore, Rex gave in. He only wanted one thing at the moment and that was to find the girls. He was more than happy to entertain a bit of give and take if it meant he would get what he wanted.

The door groaned when it was opened. Even through the thick smell of fresh smoke, the hallway still smelled sterile; the heavy door most likely acting as a barrier and preventing it from being tainted by any other scents. The sound of their shoes hitting the smooth cement echoed off the walls and made the metal doors ring. Each door they came to had a different code that needed to be entered in order to open it. When they opened the first door, they were horrified by what they saw.

The first puppet dangled in the air, halfway to the ceiling. They trained the flashlight on her. Her skin was powdered white, stark against the mix of deep and moderate greens of satin. Her cleavage pushed out along the top of the black lace, corseted dress, the hemline barely covered her bottom. Her lips were painted a ruby red and covered with a thin layer of gloss. Her eyes were closed, relaxed, and the lids showcased a white and silver shadow with a touch of sparkling green. Her chestnut hair had been smoothed back, not a strand out of place, and came to a stop in a flawlessly shaped bun. One rope wrapped around the base, holding her head high. She was posed in a near perfect pirouette; one pointed foot caressing the inside of her knee, her arms creating a circle in front of her. The rope work, her strings, were a piece of art that few had the talent to master, except they could see the pink along the edges, where the rope encircled her wrists, that was evidence of the raw and peeling skin. She hung perfectly still and took short, shallow breaths that didn't cause any disturbance; like a toy, a marionette that couldn't move without the master manipulating its strings.

With the color of her skin and the stiffness to her body, Rex would have sworn she was dead. The only thing that gave him hope about the rest of them was the slight expansion of her breastbone that indicated she was breathing. She had been the second to last to disappear and he didn't know if the earlier girls were lucky enough to have survived this long. He almost laughed out loud, more out of nervousness than anything else, at the idea that he was referring to this girl as lucky. He wanted to know if the other girls were this lucky. The only bit of luck this girl had had was that she wasn't dead.

Lucky was not his idea of what they were actually going through or what they had gone through. They were strung up in a dungeon. Made to look like human dolls. They were clearly abused, though he didn't yet know to what extent. They were mentally abused since they were kept alone, and each girl probably thought about all the others who had come before her, wondering if they were still alive. Wanting and needing to know if they were going through the same thing, just in a different room. Sitting back and waiting, wondering when and if he would end their suffering. Rex wondered how long ago they had given up hope of being rescued. When did the dream of being found die? Did they stand any chance of escape, was there any way to find their freedom once again? If the rest were still alive, Rex had just given them back their freedom, physically if nothing else. Mentally, he knew, they may never be free again.

They had already called for backup from neighboring towns but to Rex it seemed time had come to a standstill. Parker, Martin, and Frank had made their way to the next room but refused to let

Rex follow. They insisted he stay back with the volunteers, who were just barely maintaining their composure, to figure out how to lower the girl to the ground. Each rope was attached to its own wooden wheel on the wall but in no particular order. It was an insanely difficult puzzle to master as they had to make sure to lower each one a little at a time. It was a true test of patience as one wrong move could have catastrophic results.

The girls' muscles were severely strained and because of the rope holding her head they had to assume her spine was under pressure as well. It took nearly half an hour for her to be lowered enough to where people could fully support her body and head enough to let the wheels spin out. The outside help arrived just as they managed to lay her on the ground and start untangling the ropes.

At Martin's request, a few of the backup officers escorted Rex out of the house. He had expected it since he was too personally involved but he was hoping they might forget. He was thankful he had been allowed to stay this long, so he went outside without putting up too much of a fight.

He found Bobby curled up on the backseat of the patrol car like a young child. He opened the back door and slapped the bottom of his shoe. "Wake up."

Bobby jumped and opened his eyes wide. "Holy shit, you scared me. Did you get them? Did you find the girls?" His voice was filled with desperation.

For the first time in months, Rex wasn't looking at him like a suspect or as an adult. He was seeing him again as the scared child that he was. "We did. Your sister is alive."

Bobby broke down in tears and whimpered like a puppy. Rex could see the relief in his eyes and all the worry and stress came full force to the surface. It took every ounce of control he had to not do the same thing. He had spent months worrying about the girls, wondering if he had let them down. He had stressed himself out more than he ever had before thinking about how he would break the news to their parents if it came down to that. He thought he understood how they were feeling since he was a parent as well. But he had no idea. He glanced at Bobby again and frowned at his tear-streaked face. He rested his hand on the back of Bobby's shoulder and pulled him forward gently.

Bobby got out of the car and Rex pulled him forward. It wasn't often that any of the men in this town showed affection. Any other time Bobby would have been put off by it but at this moment he didn't think anything could feel better. He was vulnerable and he was letting it show. He sobbed into Rex's shoulder.

Rex heard a bit of commotion coming from the house and turned to see what was happening.

"Hey, Walker."

"Yeah," he yelled back while easing his grip on Bobby.

"Uh. We're gonna need you to come back in. You're not going to believe what we just found."

Chapter XVIII

I didn't intend to introduce new members.

Jake sat in the interview room for nearly six hours without saying a word. Rex was frustrated, annoyed, and angry. He considered himself lucky Lizbeth had only been gone for two days. Still, he wanted to be with her. All the girls were taken to the hospital for various injuries. Rex had been receiving phone calls and text messages for hours with updates on how they were all doing. So far, it seemed all of them would make a full recovery. They were being treated for physical injuries before having a psychiatric evaluation. Rex knew, and hoped the girls would come to understand it would be a long road to recovery.

He had just finished sending a text response when Jake finally spoke.

"Bobby ruined my plans, you know."

Rex didn't dare speak quite yet. He wanted Jake to tell his story the way he needed to.

"Tonight was supposed to be my night. I was moving them all to the main stage. I was finally going to prove to my sister that I'm better than she is."

The questions were burning the tip of his tongue. He wanted to ask a hundred questions at once.

"I've been working toward this night for so long. I've waited almost fifty years for this chance. One stupid, snooping kid ruined everything."

Rex was sweating. He couldn't help himself anymore. "You know we found your sister, too. Do you want to talk about her?" He wished he had the foresight to bring in a psychiatrist.

"My sister? Yeah. I'm not supposed to talk about her. Mother told me never to speak of her again."

"Your mother won't know. She's not around anymore, is she?"

"Nah. I killed that wretched bitch years ago. Buried her underneath the marionette I carved into that old tree trunk."

Every nerve tingled in Rex's body. He had been wondering for months what that carving was supposed to be. In his mind, he could see it clearly now. "Perfect. She'll never know. What's your sister's name?"

"Daisy. My mother said she named a beautiful baby girl after a beautiful flower. It makes my stomach turn. She always liked her better than me. Anyway, years ago, before she was even a teenager, my sister dove out a second story window, landed on her head. She hasn't walked or spoken since. It's fine by me. All she ever did was whine anyway.

"She used to have this collection of marionettes. My mother bought them for her, with matching dresses. She always thought she was so perfect, parading around in a little velvet dress, showing us how she could make her little puppets dance. My mother was mesmerized by her, always complimenting her and praising her. Everything she did was perfect. She was a perfect, beautiful little daisy. And then there was me, who my mother couldn't stand the sight of.

"Tonight, I was going to bring my sister into the large room. I was going to have all my beautiful puppets lined up with their freshly applied makeup, their handmade dresses. It was going to be my masterpiece. I practiced so hard. I had five of them, all ready to be strung up. I had the pulleys ready. I was going to show my sister what a real, master puppeteer can do. Five puppets all at one time. Five puppets under my control. Beautiful, dancing, perfectly made up puppets."

"What were you going to do after your showed Daisy your masterpiece?"

"I'm so glad you asked, sheriff. Obviously, I couldn't keep them around after that. I think I would have given them to my mother. Do you know how exhausting it is to keep them looking fresh? I mean, the real marionettes have permanent, painted makeup. But my puppets don't. I had to bathe them and change their clothes. I had to reapply their makeup and make sure to move them so they didn't get stiff. I had to feed them. It was becoming too much. Ah, but..." He looked at his watch and smiled at Rex. "There was one I wanted to keep. Do you know what today is, sheriff?"

"I'm sure you'll tell me."

"Today is Lizbeth's eighteenth birthday. She was my real prize for completing my goal. Today I was going to take her and make her mine."

Author's Bio

Trish recently moved across the country where she found her forever home, enjoying the desert sunshine and wildlife all year long. She was born and raised in a small town in northern Connecticut. Growing up, she was always fascinated by unsolved mysteries and true crimes as well as the psychological elements behind them. As an avid reader, her go to books are thriller/suspense, true crime, and cozy mysteries.

Author's Note

When you are finished reading, if you do not keep physical books, please consider donating your copy to your local library for their book sale or to your local prison book program.